THE MORNING
AND
THE EVENING

Joan Williams

THE MORNING
AND
THE EVENING

Atheneum New York

1961

A portion of this novel originally appeared,
in different form,
in The Atlantic Monthly

THE MORNING
AND
THE EVENING

I

The owner-manager was also the ticket seller and ticket taker and would have been his own projectionist, too, if labor regulations had not forced him to hire a licensed one. He did not take his first customer for a loony and tried to charge him full admission.

The man next in line said quietly, "He don't usually pay but half fare."

The owner looked at his customer warily then; he did not look like a loony, was tall, thin, stoop-shouldered, with a weather-beaten face that seemed to know all about struggle and with eyes that looked as if he were thinking, even as if he were looking for something; they weren't empty, like the eyes of most loonies. The eyes were what fooled him.

He was hesitant: they might be trying to pull some kind of deal. You couldn't ever tell. He'd been taking his movie around in the back country for three years and didn't understand these people

3

yet. Why'd they live in country like this, bother with the little they eked out of it?

Then the loony tried to say something, opened his mouth, and nothing came out except saliva. It drooled on his pink, hanging lip a minute, then ran down his chin and dropped onto his shirt when he moaned.

The owner followed the loony's eyes, and finally he took the thin sweaty dime out of his uncurled hand.

The loony hoisted up his overalls strap and went toward the tent. The owner looked after him, still wary: he'd had trouble with too many loonies after they got into the show. "How long's he been that way?" he said.

The man next in line looked at his wife. "Reckon 'bout forty years?" he said.

"Reckon so," she said; "long's however old he is."

The man turned back. "Reckon 'bout forty years," he said.

The owner tore off two tickets, took the man's forty cents. "Think he's liable to cause any trouble?" he asked cautiously.

The man turned to his wife. "Don't reckon so, do you?" he said.

"No," she said, still standing where she was. "Might just moan a little."

"Naw, might jist moan a little," said the man, going on toward the tent, his wife going along behind.

When he had filled all the campstools in the

tent, lined the kids up around the sides, the owner told the rest to come back tomorrow night and went inside. Christ, it was stuffy and smelled. He walked along the little aisle left in the sawdust, feeling their eyes in the dark watching him expectantly. When he got to the small white screen set up in front, he turned. "Joe, a light," he said.

The projection man at the back of the tent threw the spotlight on him, and a chorus of oh's rose from the crowd. The light came from behind a piece of cardboard with holes covered over by red and green and blue cellophane, so that it played across the owner's face like a rainbow. "Ain't that the berries," he said, smiling out.

He could see only those sitting along the aisle where the light came; he noted where the loony sat—second aisle seat on the right. "Now, don't worry," the owner said. "I'm not going to make a speech." He paused and everybody laughed. "I just want to tell you how glad I am to be back here," he went on, still smiling. "All the places I go, I tell that the finest folks I ever met are in Marigold, Mississippi, and from one summer till the next I look toward getting back here. So I just had to say these few words. Thank you all for coming, and I hope you like the show. Let 'er go, Joe," he said, and went to sit down.

But the light didn't go off, it just kept on playing where his face had been, only now against the white, silent screen. Everybody waited. "Joe," the owner said, wiping his forehead.

Finally somebody in the rear said, "He's outside smoking."

"Well, couldn't you tell him to come in?" the owner said.

"Reckon so," the voice said. The tent flap was lifted, and everybody looked at the thin blue line of twilight showing, commented on how no air came in. "The man says for you to come on in and get the picture started."

A red glow showed against the blue, then Joe flipped away his cigarette and closed the flap. He cut off the spotlight, started the little black box whirring, and threw the movie beam where the spotlight beam had been. Only, he threw it too high. Black and white words slid across the tent top upside down, while thin jumpy music began to play. Everybody sat quietly; no one would laugh, except the owner himself. He jumped up from his seat toward the side, where he could keep an eye on things, laughing nervously. "Just a minute, folks, everything'll get straightened out," he said, waving them back down as if someone had thought of leaving. It was quiet while the projection man clicked off the whirring, then started it again. The light beam came like sundust down the aisle, and the title and the thin music came from the screen this time. There was a rustle while everybody got settled (no one would move much after the picture started) and a steady drone of voices, reading off what the titles said to those who didn't know.

The owner went back and sat down. He leaned back into the dark and had himself a good quiet laugh. "Oh, my God," he said to himself when he had finished and had taken out his handkerchief and was wiping his forehead. He'd seen the loony leaning way down off his campstool, almost on his head, watching the movie on the tent top.

Jake straightened up when the writing disappeared. He didn't know where it or the music had gone. No one else moved, so he sat quietly and folded his hands. He remembered the man who didn't want to take his dime, and saw him looking at him and laughing. So he grinned back. But the man's face went back into the dark. Then he heard the sound again, a whirring as a snake made when he tried to pick it up, and he looked for it on the tent top.

"There," the thin little girl next to him whispered, and she put her hand on his face and pulled it down, pointed it frontward.

The unexpected touch of the hand coming out of the dark sent him bolt upright. He stared straight ahead at the words, without seeing them. Then he sat back, let himself feel again how the hand had felt: soft.

Softness he understood.

The dark, the movie, the people around were lost to him now while he was remembering softness. One thing at a time he could know.

Some things he had learned: repeated things. And some things he knew instinctively, animal-like: tones, touches, whether they were kind, or not.

The child's hand had touched him as his mother's did whenever he put his head in her lap and she held his face close. It touched him as his mother's had done when she gave him the dime.

He always wanted to hold hands when they touched him this way. But his mother had pulled back. "Now don't," she had said. "Now don't." When he tried to put his arm around her then, she had run, saying brokenly, "Oh, God, don't let him want to do that. Maybe you oughtn't to go. Naw, naw, you can go, don't cry." She had followed him as far as the gate. "But don't touch nobody, Jake. Don't *touch* nobody," she said all the time he was going down the road, as she had said so many times before.

Remembering, because it hadn't been too long, Jake did not try to find the hand in the dark now.

The movie music had begun softly at first, but now it came loud and thin, came to him slowly; then he began to listen, and there was nothing else. It came to him beautiful and sourceless and bird-like, filled the tent, and he heard it not with his ears, but way inside him. In the pit of his stomach he heard it and tasted with it his supper, the sour, warm taste of corn bread and buttermilk.

Then, as always when something moved him, the music began to creep up inside him, and he tightened his legs together. "Jake," his mother had said before he left, "if you got to go, go outside behind a tree. Please, God, let him."

He held himself rigid on the narrow campstool and continued to listen.

The music was in his chest now, hurting. It would move on up to his mouth, then it would be soundless—he knew. He knew he had to catch it before it was soundless. He waited in the dark for the right moment, while the music sang to him as the birds do before they fly away.

"Caw, caw," the little boys would cry when Jake reached up after the birds. "I'm a bird, Jake. Catch *me*."

The music rose, and it seemed to Jake soaring, going away. This was the moment, and he began to run after it, and it seemed so close he thought this time he had caught it. Then something held him and he turned, looked into the face he had seen before with colors on it, and the owner dragged him, pushed him into his seat roughly. "Stay down, Jake," everyone called.

He felt the water running down his leg, but he sat still. The music had ceased, and he had forgotten it. He simply found himself, without surprise, sitting in the dark, as often he seemed to wake from a long sleep and find himself places, and he felt if he sat quietly long enough, it would come to him why he was there. But the small voice next to him soon whispered in his ear, "Look at the pictures."

Then Jake became aware of the picture before him, and he looked at it, began to fit things together piecemeal: two men were on the white sheet; they were on horses; they held guns and pointed them in the air toward hills; one took off a big, wide hat, put it on again; they tied something over their faces. The men began to talk and Jake watched the movements of their mouths beneath the masks; he could tell when their mouths were opening and closing. He listened carefully, bent forward on his stool to hear them better.

He heard what they said, heard each one. One said something and he heard him distinctly; then the other said something and he heard him, but then he could not remember what the first had said. He started over again. He leaned forward more, watched and listened carefully to each man; would begin to think what one had said when the other would speak—and he turned his head quickly and began to think what *he* was saying. There was not enough time, and he began to feel the tightness coming on again.

People, sometimes even his mother, always spoke to him too fast. They said a word and he began to think about it, but when they continued to say words, it all became a jumble. He tried again and again to go back to the first word, but too many others had come between, and even his first faint glimmer would be gone. If there was time, he felt he could know what was said; he was sure. Often he felt that if only he had time, he could even answer.

For he felt words inside him the way he felt music. The words came to him, starting in his stomach, and he listened to them carefully while they moved on up to his chest, began to hurt him; then in a rush the words would be in his mouth, and he would open it. He would hear the sounds he made and would be sure he had said the words clearly, and he would smile proudly; but he knew he had not when they looked away and said, "Wipe off your mouth, Jake."

On the screen the two men went riding away suddenly toward the hills; the music came again very loud. Jake jerked up to listen, but it was not the bird music. This music went *pound pound pound,* faster and faster. It went galloping loud. It rose out of the dark and sounded terribly in his head. It went *thumpty thumpty thump,* louder and faster, came closer and closer, and he felt it was coming after him; there was no time to run from the tent. He screwed his eyes shut and pulled his head into his shoulders, held his hands over his ears hard. He ran within himself now, as he did when the little boys chased him, beating tin pails with rocks.

"I'm a bird, Jake. Listen to the birdies," the little boys would yell, running after him, beating horribly. And he would run crazily for miles, holding his ears, and long after he outran them he still heard the poundings, and not until he came to a place that was quiet and had sat for a long time could he take down his hands; then he would cry, rubbing his ears. Now he began to cry. "Shut up that noise, Jake," several of the men called out behind him in the dark.

One of the ladies leaned toward the owner. "He always tries to sing when he hears music," she explained. The movie man nodded condescendingly.

Jake stopped crying when the men yelled at him. He understood the tone of their voices. The music quieted, faded, but he sat bent over on his campstool with his head down, his hands still holding his ears.

The men spoke to him in the same tone whenever he saw them in town, leaning back in straight-legged chairs against the store fronts, hounds sleeping in circles at their feet. He had long wanted a dog; he would stop to ask the men where he could get one. As he leaned over to pat the soft warm bellies of their hounds, he would begin to tell them how he wanted a dog, too. Banging their chair legs to the porch, they would jump up and yell, "Get on away, Jake. Get him away from *my* bitch. Get on, stop that there moanin'."

Then he would take himself away, telling them he would come back tomorrow to find out where he could get him a dog.

"Wake up, Jake." Behind him, a man caught hold of his overalls, jerked him up. His eyes opened, astonished. He saw the tent over his head, felt the people around him in the dark, was aware of a mosquito; he remembered something had jerked him, a voice had said something. He listened to the breathing around him.

Between the light coming down the aisle he saw faces, all looking straight ahead. He looked ahead too. He saw the picture, remembered he had seen it before, and realized mutely that this was why he was there, to look at the picture. He looked at it intently.

But he felt tired, as if he had been running for a long time; he couldn't think what the picture was —it was only black-and-white shadows. His mouth fell open and he stared straight ahead of himself.

The thin childish voice next to him began to whisper in his ear quietly, slowly, "They're riding over the hill to rustle the cows. They're the badmen."

Jake nodded his head slowly with each word, shook it at the last.

His mother had primed him. She sat him down for a long time before he came and told him what he would see; having been to the movie three summers ago, she knew. "You'll like the cows, the horses, the hills," she said, and made him nod his head. "But not the badmen." Then she made him shake it. His mother never let him talk, though he wanted to. "You don't have to talk, son," she would say. "You don't have to. Be quiet now."

It was hotter than ever in the tent now, as if

twenty-five people sitting still for an hour had breathed up all the air. Next to the child a woman began to fan herself, and when she leaned around and fanned the child too, Jake felt a small breeze; he let himself feel it and smell the smell that came with it, sweet, the way his mother smelled when she put powder on her face.

The woman looked away and he followed her gaze. He saw a man riding a horse, coming slowly down a road. Everyone in the crowd began to clap; the little boys in the back whistled. Jake smiled, then he laughed, cupped his big pawlike hands together and pulled them apart, made a slapping sound like everyone else. He watched his hands going together, coming apart, making a noise; then the little-girl voice whispered, "Quit now," and he quit.

He looked where the little girl looked, watched the man on the horse again. The man opened his mouth and began to sing. Jake rocked back and forth on his campstool as the man rocked back and forth on his horse, and he heard the singing inside him, smiling to himself. He had known for a long time that he could sing. Whenever he was alone he would sing, but he kept it a secret.

The man sang loudly and Jake grinned now, knowing the sounds in him to be the same as the man made. When the child next to him, lost in the movie, leaned against his shoulder, he turned and looked at her face, small, perspiring, open-mouthed; he saw her breath going in time to the music, and he remembered her voice touching his ear, her hand touching his face a long time ago, and it came to him suddenly to tell her he could sing. Softly, with closed eyes, he began to sing, wanting just this one small face to know his secret. Abruptly the face hissed close to his, snakelike, "Shhh, you shut up that moanin'," and he felt a breeze beat in his face very hard. He opened his eyes and looked into an angry face with a tongue shooting out like the snake's did, with eyes that were two hard slits. The woman had jerked the little girl away, was there in her place.

Jake turned away frightened, hunched up on his stool, keeping himself away, his song forgotten. Was he supposed to run? He did not know. He sat on in the dark, trembling until his back began to ache so he had to move. Cautiously he slid his feet from under the stool, gradually straightened his cramped legs; the face didn't turn on him. Stealthily then he eased out his back, sat up. Over the head in front of him he saw the movie again.

A man got off a horse, went up to a girl, stroked her long hair, talking softly. Jake's eyes followed the stroking up and down, and slowly his fingers began to curl, uncurl, against the rough knee of his overalls.

"Shh, shh," the snake face said. Jake jumped, but

the face was not looking at him; it was turned toward the back where the little boys hooted like owls.

He watched the stroking again—soft, soft, he knew, remembering Sarah Jane. He began to ache, remembering Sarah Jane.

"Sarah Jane, Sarah Jane," he would moan softly over and over, stroking her. And she never moved, she never pulled away from him. She just listened to him. When he had finished all he had to say, she would look at him with unwavering eyes. Spent with telling at last, he would sit down then and, leaning his head into her stomach, begin to milk her. When the sweet, warm milk came, he would sometimes begin to cry, because of the stillness and the listening that was Sarah Jane; he would tell her then how she was the only one who would listen. But soon his mother would come running down to the cowshed, screaming, "Get away from her now, Jake. Get away!" And she would take him away. All the time going to the house he tried to tell her about Sarah Jane, but she would say, "Hush now, hush." Then he would cry, looking back at Sarah Jane watching him with her calm brown eyes.

When the man stopped stroking, Jake's fingers hesitated, half curled. He sat waiting, but the screen flickered, the scene changed, and the man was gone. There were horses instead, pounding frightfully going over a hill, and the sound of gunshots. Not only the next face but all the faces hissed, and twenty-five pairs of feet thudded dully against the sawdust. Jake laughed, picked up one of his feet, then the other, set each down in the sawdust, stomping too.

Suddenly through a cloud of dust on the screen, he saw a cow face come toward him with wild frightened eyes, mooing loudly and mournfully. He stood up. "Sarah Jane, Sarah Jane," he cried out, a gaunt figure waving mute and frantic arms before the onrushing herd of cattle.

"Sarah Jane, Sarah Jane," he called again and again, beginning to run. The owner grabbed him by his crossed straps and one sleeve, dragged him down the light beam through the aisle of snickering faces, and out into the night. "God damn you, loon," he muttered.

Jake pulled back toward the tent, but the man shook him hard; then Jake forgot about the tent. He stood bewildered, with the man's face breathing close to his. "You're not getting back in there," the owner gritted out between his teeth.

With no thought left of what was inside the tent, Jake stood limply while the owner held him. Finally the owner released him and lit a cigarette, stood facing him, waiting to overcome his anger. "Just God damn you," he said as he drew on the cigarette, which glowed faintly red against his face in the dark.

And this faint red glow stirred up, as much as possible, a memory in Jake. When he had seen the owner with the spotlight playing across his face, he had associated it with the one thing of color indelibly etched on his mind—the sunset—because he watched it daily, and now he knew that he had seen this face before with color on it. He began to tell the man. "Take your hands off me. Get on away," the owner said, giving him a good shove before he threw away his cigarette and went on back into the tent.

Jake turned after him, knew from the tone of his voice not to follow, and stood holding on to the outside fold of the tent flap, beginning to tell the man about the sun going down red against a darkening sky. In a little while someone stuck his head out. "Shut up that noise and go home," he said, and while the tent flap was open Jake glimpsed a man and a girl, heard music, saw a horse with its mane waving in the wind; then he was staring at nothing, with his nose up against the closed flap of the tent.

He turned, ran his hand over his nose where the rough tent had scratched it, and went on slowly down the faint road. The moon came out smiling from behind a cloud, opened up a white path; he followed it, listening to the staccato sounds from katydids hiding in the tall grass alongside the road, listening to the shrill loud screaming of locusts from somewhere overhead, listening to the stumbling craunch of his own feet on the gravel, all sounds.

Alone, he began to call up words from way inside him. A bird fluttered in one of the poplar trees, and he looked for it between the white leaves. It

18

sang sleepily way up, and he went on. He went instinctively, not having to think where he was going. Because it was quiet the words came easily but formed slowly, one by one, and he waited for them to come as he walked.

When he had been in the quiet for about a mile, he began to remember: music. He stored up words to go with the music. After a while he remembered the horse, and he stored up words to go with the horse. He remembered the wind.

He turned out of the moonlight and went through the dark again, his feet following surely the thin side road.

When he saw the little house, with one lighted window, he went up to it and looked inside. A woman knelt by a bed, and he watched her. As she stood up and got into bed, he saw without surprise that it was his mother and knew he was home. His mother sat in the bed by the lamp and he knew she was waiting for him. He waited, watching her. The night sounds continued around him; they had become part of his hearing now, and he did not have to listen to them consciously. With the sounds around him, with the words inside him, he felt again the uncontrollable thing that guided him, and he wanted to make sounds too. He moved his hands out in a sweeping gesture, stood outside the window, nodded his head up and down, shook it once.

But the words still stirred him, wanting to be said. Suddenly he found himself going away from the window, and he went, went as if he were following himself.

He went quietly through the tall, dew-wet grass, felt it itch his leg, but he forgot it before he could remember to stop and scratch. He went on with the words carefully inside him. The music began, churned inside him with the words, words about the horse with its mane waving in the wind, and he held everything inside him together as much as he could, till the moment to tell them.

He found himself at the gate, lifted it and set it back in its rut. Then he went silently, smelling the ragweed, heard frog music, and he heard it and set it apart slowly from his own music. Instinctively he went on through the dark and circled wide around the place where he had seen the snake.

As he went down into the summer-dried ditch, came up again, the words jarred loose from his chest and he started running, telling them.

As he heard the first faint bell tinkle, he was running faster, telling about the wind, waving his arms.

He smelled the pasture for the first time as he came up to her, and he lay down immediately with his head on her soft flank. When he felt her stillness and her warm breath smelling of grass, he began to tell her about the music, and he knew, as much as he could, that through the long summer he would come here again and again.

2

Jake's mother, standing at the kitchen window, saw him come up out of the potato cellar beneath the house, trip over the top of the ladder, and hit his chin sharply on a rock as he fell to the ground. But before she could move, he had gotten up. In one swift, unusual, sure movement, he collected the spilled potatoes.

Like one of those cartoon shows, she thought, when things spilled out of a person's arms jump back into them.

The blow on the chin had been quite hard, she saw now that he was directly beneath the window. Blood had appeared where the skin had broken open and a faintly blue lump had formed. He seemed either not to mind or to be completely oblivious to what had happened. His expression never changed. It was altogether concentrated on carrying the potatoes for her. He brought them up the back steps and dropped them into a basket. She smelled faintly the odor of dirt that arose from them. Then he went away again, down the back steps.

Soup simmering on the wood stove rattled the lid of its iron pot. Corn bread was baking in the oven. She stood in the kitchen full of heat and steam and thought of that dark cool cellar in the earth out of which Jake had just come. She would like to go down there and stay a long time, with perhaps a candle to light it by night. The fear of it she had once felt had passed gradually after so many years.

The wooden door of the cellar was of two parts that opened outward, and flush to the ground. It was thirty years ago she had gone down into the cellar and left one side of the door closed and locked on the outside. She had been in the farthest reaches selecting potatoes when suddenly she was closed completely into the earth.

Terrified, she had turned, and all she could see was a faint crack of daylight that was the outline of the door.

"Jake!" she had called.

But the same instinct which made her call made her call hollowly, tonelessly, and not loud enough for him to hear; he did not know how to open the door, and he did not know how to close and lock it either.

Dropping potatoes, she put her hands out blindly to the dark and made her way through it, across the damp earth floor, at each step feeling snakes slithering toward her worn and split-open shoes. She found the ladder and gripped it and went up quickly to the top. She crouched, her face as close as possible to the crack of daylight: security now and life itself. Once, she pushed without hope at the unyielding weight of the door.

It was early morning. There would be no strangers on the place at this hour. To whoever had closed the door, this was home.

"Jud!" she called loudly to her oldest son.

It seemed she heard heavy breathing on the other side of the door. But she could not be sure and told herself afterward it was only imagination.

She drifted into semisleep, and heard the stealthy unsliding of the bolt. Half asleep, half awake, she argued with herself over whether she had heard it or dreamed it, and suddenly she was wide awake knowing she had heard it. She pushed violently with all her weight against the door; unnecessarily, for it came easily open.

Dazed and blinking, she came into the bright sunlight. For a moment she stared about foolishly at the familiar and spring-filled countryside with a feeling that she should not have recognized it.

On the back steps Jake sat in the sun, alternately patting the heads of Jud's two hounds. So Jud is back from hunting, she thought.

She went slowly toward Jake, watching as the hounds, their whole behinds wagging, pushed their noses against his hands. When her shadow overcame him, he looked up. Warmth and recognition came into his eyes. She leaned close and smoothed back his hair. "You can feed them," she said softly, and made appropriate gestures so that he understood her. He came alive and went up the back steps for the coarse white cornmeal bread she baked weekly for the dogs; it was kept in a blue enamel pan on the back porch. He broke off large pie-shaped wedges and came back and fed the dogs out of his hands.

She had followed him up the steps. Jud was whistling inside his room, and she went down the hall to it. His boots were on the front porch beside the door; the door was slightly ajar, as if he had just come in that way, from the road and the town. He stood before the mirror of his highboy removing the clothes he had been out in all night.

"Did you get anything?" she said.

He drew his shirt over his head and then from his arms. "Those damn dogs," he said. "Ran a fox all night as close as from here to the porch and never did catch up to him."

"Jake's feeding them now," she said.

"Oh sh——," he said, the sound in his throat afterward one of disgust.

Anger, cold as a chill, ran through her. But she would not say anything. She was afraid to. She stared, newly aware of his strong arms and the muscles like taut cords across his chest and stomach. The thought of this enormous strength and what he could do with it made her feel sick. It was with wonder she thought back to the time when she had carried him inside her. It seemed impossible that any-

24

thing as large as he could have ever been a baby. She remembered that the first time she held him, a great bunch of pink roses had been beside the bed. A petal had fallen from one onto the table. Picking it up, she had wrapped his tiny fist completely inside it. She had thought, I always want to remember this, that his fist fit inside a rose petal.

She said, "Will you go to the cellar for potatoes? I thought I saw a snake in it and run back up. I just want about five. Just enough for potato salad at noon."

Watching his face, she thought it remained as coldly expressionless as always, except, perhaps, for a slight shifting of his eyes away from her.

"Yeah," he said. "I'll go." And he made a great show of taking the poker in case he saw the snake.

Before he went under the house he hesitated, and she wondered if he was considering that she might, in turn, lock him up. Would he open both sides of the door, or dare risk leaving one side locked? Curious as she was, she was afraid to go outside and look. Suppose he turned on her out of fear? His fear would be more dangerous than the hate she believed caused the other incident. How many times had he told her, I hate this town, and this place, and Jake!

She did not believe he truly hated her. But she was the reason he had to stay at home. It was as if he had wanted her to know just how much he meant it when he said he hated those things; as if he had had to get back at something, she thought.

25

She did not remember much more, in detail, of that afternoon almost thirty years ago, except that much later she had had to go onto the porch and tell Jake to leave the dogs and come inside. It had begun to lighten and to drizzle rain.

Jud, she thought, had been such a handsome boy! At the window she watched Jake again. He had stopped the bleeding of his chin against his shirt sleeve. Now he was headed toward the pasture. She would let him go. She was too tired to bring him in and clean him up. Walking away from her, he was thin and slight and angular, where Jud had been massive. She had never seen any resemblance between the two of them until a few nights ago when Jake came home from the picture show. When she got into bed, she had glanced at the window just as he looked in. His face framed by the night behind him had been lit in the center by the lamp indoors. His eyes usually were squinted, their color impossible to see; but staring, they had widened, and she had seen as if for the first time that they were the same clear white-blue color as Jud's. His nose, caught in shadows, had had something to its bridge that reminded her of Jud's handsome aquiline one. Though Jake's looked as if it had been broken, she thought, or pushed aside. It just missed being, not perfect, but all right. Like him, she thought, near tears, like most everything about him.

She wanted to go to the door and call him back from the pasture. Repeatedly she dreamed, until it

26

had become almost real, that Sarah Jane had turned into an enormous pawing bull, with great horns and flame-filled nostrils. And Jake was walking toward her, his hands outstretched to scratch between her ears. When she woke, her nightclothes would always be as wet as if drenched by rain. The feeling would hang on that something dreadful had happened to Jake. And unaccountably she had had the feeling the night he looked in on her after the picture show. She had gotten out of bed and walked to the door and called him. But he had gone. She went back to bed and lay awake, fearful and waiting. Then long afterward she heard in town the starting up of many motors and knew the show had just let out. Why had Jake come home so early? All that time she had been lying awake waiting to find out, without knowing it. She waited the night through for a knock at the door and someone to tell her, but no one ever came. And no one had told her at any time afterward. She comforted herself with the thought that whatever it was, it was not as bad as it could have been.

It was her belief that Jake was as he was as punishment for the one infidelity of her life. It had happened several years before he was born, in the summertime, with the leader of a revival meeting that had come to town for two weeks. She had been drawn to the man from her first sight of him. And the second week of the revival she had realized that just as she had stared at him longingly, distantly, so now night after night he stared at her. The Sunday afternoon before the final meeting that night, she had come to the church as if by prearrangement, though she had no recollection of ever having spoken to him alone. He had been there. Everything was over very quickly. But it had been the surprise and delight of her life to find herself the woman she had been in that instant. She would never be the same again; she knew that. She had walked out of the church that afternoon with a great burden of guilt upon her, but not regret; she had learned too much. She had wanted to turn around and nod to him as he stood at the window watching her; but she had thought, If I do, I'll see he's just a man. And the memory was as if she had been in touch with God Himself, or been brushed with gold by angel's wings.

When Jake was born some years later, it was out of this greater measure of love that she bore him for her husband, Cecil, and out of it that she loved them both. But before Jake was a year old, Cecil died; he came from a line of people who did not live past sixty, and she had not expected him to. Still, it was a great shock the day he walked through the front gate and dropped dead just short of his fiftieth birthday. Afterward when she thought of their life together, she thought it had been all right. Their marriage had fallen early into a pattern from which it seldom deviated. When it was daylight, they had gotten up; when it was dark, they had gone to bed.

The hours between, they worked the farm. Their lives had been exactly like those of the whole community except for slight variations: people were born, died, took sick and got married at different times. A few met unexpected accidents. One young couple even got a divorce, and once Miss Alma, Miss Rubye Brown, Selma Murphy and some others had taken a bus tour to Williamsburg and New York City; they said another summer they would go out West, to San Francisco, Salt Lake City, Seattle and Lake Louise, but they never did. Sometimes she felt only her own life was any different, and it was Jake that made it so.

After Cecil's death, she did the farm work with only Jud's help; he was then eleven, ten years older than Jake. At first she put down to this difference in age Jud's behavior to Jake. She thought it was normal that he be jealous and resentful, but what was not normal was his scornful laughter. Whatever Jake did, Jud laughed.

Jake had walked late and was slow about everything, but she excused away even his not learning to talk. The one thing finally she could not excuse away was what she had seen this morning: his imperviousness to hurt. If he fell, he did not cry. Whatever his cut, scratch, bruise, however much blood he shed, he seemed unaware of it. Eventually, when it was confirmed that something was wrong with him, she believed Jud had known it all along, that he had some instinct peculiar to animals and children alike, sensed what was weaker, imperfect, unable to escape him and was, therefore, his prey. She believed also that Jake's inability to feel hurt was God's compensation for what else He had done.

One day after she had been sick for a long time, Jake's inabilities were definitely established. A Negro, Lou, had been living in to do the work. She had not said a word about Jake, but the mother had seen her watching him and the words right ready on Lou's lips to confirm any suspicions the mother might voice. Then it was her first day out of bed. Impatient with her long idleness, she had been in the kitchen rolling out dough for the noon biscuits when she heard Lou come in behind her and stand. Without turning, she said, "You want something, Lou?"

"He fallen off the bed again. Bad, this time," Lou said, softly.

After a moment, she said, "Did he cry?"

"No'm," Lou said.

She had dampened the dough and rolled it over the pin again securely before she left it. Afterward, wondering why she had taken that time, she thought it was that she had wanted so much for something to go right.

She found him lying on his back, staring up at the ceiling, blood gushing like a small fountain out of his head where he had struck the iron bed post in falling. They had had to carry him to the doctor that time; then there was no more room for doubt.

The sins of the parents. The words haunted her over and over in the car going home. When she was alone she cried, But why not me? why wasn't I crippled or maimed or made to lose my senses?

She considered saying it was the blow on the head that made him the way he was. But she remembered Lou's knowing and compassionate looks and knew that she could not. She remembered the looks of others that she would not acknowledge before and now had to, and knew that she could not. "Just don't let 'em pity me," she said.

"Jesus H. God!" Jud had said. "First, I got to be born in this little town, to this stinking farm, and now this!"

He had pointed to the hurt child huddled like a heap of old rags, bandaged now and unmoving, lying on the farthest reaches of the bed, against the wall.

Looking at Jud's face, she had thought, It ain't just that he's a grown man at fourteen. It's that he's a bitter old one.

But she said only, "Don't use His name that way."

To her annoyance she found that now she spied on Jud. She watched to see how he treated the littlest chicks in the brood and the runt of his bitch's litter. He showed no distaste, however, even for a rooster that developed a gigantic and unsightly goiter. She saw him once step over a bug crossing the road. He drowned a kitten born with only two feet, but that was merciful, she thought.

She did her best about Jake: kept him clean, trained him as much as he could be trained and taught him as much as he could learn. When he was older, she let him go about as freely as she would have any child.

One day Jud came home from town, embarrassed, yelling, "Keep that bastard home!"

"He ain't no bastard," she said.

"All right—idiot!" he said: a word that hurt her worse, and she knew he knew it.

Afterward whenever he spoke of Jake he would say, "That blithering, slobbering . . ."

And before he could finish, she would cry, "Hush! Oh my God, hush!"

"Well, keep him home then," he would say.

"But why?" she said finally. "Why? He ain't some dumb animal to be penned up."

"Oh?" he had said. "Ain't he?"

That time she said, "What is it you want, Jud?"

"To go," he said, simply. "Just to go. To get as far as I can away from here and this little town and him. Woman, I want to see something."

Cecil would have told him not to holler at his momma, she thought. Aloud, she had said, "Well, go."

"Oh, Ma," he had said. "I ain't just plumb rotten. How can I just go off and leave you with nobody?"

"I got somebody," she said.

"Oh sh——," he said.

She did not want him to go. At night she lay awake asking herself, How can I keep him here? How much longer is he going to stay?

In the room next to hers she would sometimes hear a whimper in sleep from the mute child. In winter she would lie awake listening to his troubled adenoidal breathing; he always had a cold. She would strain toward any noise in the other part of the house, always imagining Jud creeping from one of the low windows of the house with all his possessions. If an acorn or a pecan fell with a crack to the ground she was sure it was his heavy feet treading it. Winter wind rattling the panes sent her bolt upright in bed listening for the stealthy opening of the window afterward. Mornings when she woke and heard Jud coughing or spitting or sometimes whistling in his room, she was glad.

No mother wants to be left, she told herself. It's all right to want him here long as I don't do nothing to keep him.

When Cecil died, Jud had had to quit school. She often thought things might have been better if that had not happened; though the truth was, and she suspected it, that left to his own devices, Jud would not have gone on to the next grade anyway. Though in later years when he began to feel his lack of education, he blamed everything on that; he said he had never had a chance.

The years went by and Jake grew. She and Jud

worked, but the farm did not grow. It remained about the same, sometimes slipping a little, gradually recovering.

Jud's friends had become the worst boys in the county: the ones who smoked behind the schoolhouse if they went to school, and anywhere if they did not; who drank when they could get something, took Negro girls as a lark and otherwise told impossible tales of their prowess with white ones. The room he lived in became almost a separate part of the house. When he was not at home, the door was closed and locked. She was allowed in to clean only when he was there. He would sit on the bed, watching from the corner of his eye each flick of her dust cloth, ostensibly reading a comic strip in a ten-cent "big-little" book. She had no suspicions about what she might find in his room; often she wondered what it was he thought she was looking for.

Jake stayed in what she had come to think of as their part of the house: his room and her room and the kitchen. She grew accustomed to his being about, the way one does to a dog or cat; having to dress, feed, care for him was like playing a child's game with a doll. She talked aloud to him as lonely people do to animals, continually and intimately, and because he could neither respond nor understand, she had the pleasure of sharing her innermost secrets with him; yet she retained them. To her surprise, she noticed one day that he was listening. He nodded and smiled and his eyes never left her face. She broke off her sentence and stared. Then she smiled. She reached over and patted his knee. Then she nodded for him to follow. They went into the kitchen and she fixed a pot of tea and set it between them. In this manner, filling and refilling their cups, he nodding and smiling, she talking, they fell into the habit of reviewing their whole day's happenings.

He followed her outside at five, as usual—he followed her almost everywhere. Except to Jud's room, she thought suddenly, turning around and looking at him; and no one had ever told him not to. On impulse, she thrust the feed sack forward into his hands. He stared at her. But it was not with a look of ignorance at all, but rather one of recognition of her recognition. She thought a look of relief passed across his face. He went straight to the chickens and scattered their feed about in exactly the right proportions. His mouth moved the while and his throat worked convulsively.

He's trying to say, Here chick, chick, she thought.

She went to the steps, put her head in her lap, and cried. It was for the first time since Cecil died.

She did not mention it to Jud. The next afternoon when he was home, she simply handed the sack to Jake. She saw Jud was at first surprised and then seemingly both glad and angry. She found other things for Jake to do. One day she told everybody in town proudly, "He's a good fetcher and toter."

35

Everyone, glad of her happiness, patted Jake and smiled, and he grinned back. He came to know those words: fetcher and toter. When she said them, he grinned and nodded and in some way, everyone was aware, congratulated himself.

Jud was beginning to lose meaning for her, and her love was transposing. Sometimes she felt he had already moved away. No longer allowed into his room, she no longer saw his boyishly rumpled head on the pillow. She did not straighten his covers or dwell over the impression on the bed where he had slept his deep youthful sleep. When she touched his clothes, it was only to wash them; the pockets had already been emptied. They could have been the clothes of a stranger. He had selected and bought them himself, without even her knowledge. When he was away from home, it was as if he had never been there.

"You'd think having his room locked up all day, there'd be some smell of him to it when it was open," she told Jake.

But there was nothing of him about, not a smell of tobacco or hair tonic or shaving cream. No smell of him even clung to his clothes. It was as if the coldness about him had killed everything.

She depended on the familiarity of Jake, on the warmth of the room after he had bathed in it and the smell of Octagon, the soap he liked. The smell of the feed sack clung to his clothes and the musky smell of the corn he fed the chickens. There was

36

about him later the smell of shaving lather when he finally grew a slight beard and she shaved him. Often there was the smell of food about him. He spilled it and she could not get him clean again until that smell had become part of her memory of him, too. When she kissed him, his breath had a warmth to it and a smell slightly like gravy, like the breath of small puppies.

Then Jud was going. She was still shut out of his room, but somehow she knew on that day that behind the closed door he was packing. She imagined how he would look picking and choosing among his things, reluctant to part with anything. She knew what he would decide on and what he would have to leave. She wondered what to do afterward with all the things he had tacked on his walls, with the baseballs and gloves, the pictures of old girl friends.

He would have to leave the slick black-and-white nickel pictures that had been on the walls so long now they curled away from them: baseball boys, their peaked caps pulled low; the baseball king, what's his name? she thought. And the two good-looking fighters, the Tunney boy and Jack Dempsey—somehow she had always thought all fighters had permanently mangled ears and noses and almost-closed eyes. He even had a picture of a Negro on the wall. When she asked about it he said, "He beat out the Heinie, didn't he?" But she had secretly hoped no one else who came to the house would notice it. He even had a few pictures of movie stars; one was of Johnny Mack Brown, to whom she was partial herself.

She wondered if Jud would take his guitar, and sat waiting to see. She thought of how the room would look after he left, strewn but empty.

When he opened the door, he had the guitar. Her impulse was to say, "That's going to be a bulk to carry, Son."

On the other hand she did not want to have to send it to him. He would want it and he would not be back. She knew that. Though when he opened the door and saw her, he looked sheepish. He said, "I'm going, Ma. But I'll be back so much you'll say, 'Why don't he make up his mind whether he's coming or going.' And you'll be coming to Memphis, somehow."

"Memphis!" she said. "I haven't been to Memphis in ten years and don't expect to go. All that noise! I'd be so nervous I'd be fit to be tied. I'm not getting any younger, you know. I'm forty-three years old."

"I'm not gettin' any younger either, you know," he said, quietly.

"I guess none of us are," she said. "So go on and go, before it's too late."

"It ain't ever going to be too late," he said. "I always was and I always will be going to go."

"Well, go on then," she said, "while I'm still alive to take care of him."

38

What would happen after that hung unasked between them. But only a moment, for Jud bent and picked up the valise he had set down and went to the door. She followed him to the edge of the porch and stood as he stepped off it and went down the short path to the gate. He half spoke over his shoulder, half turned around.

"So long, Ma," he said.

She watched him walk off down the winter-rutted road and thought, It sure would make a whole lot of difference if he did get rich.

She thought, Suppose he got on the stage with that guitar. He was good with that guitar; he could even make up tunes himself.

She turned away from the sight of his powerful strong shoulders and his broad back going off down the road. He was carrying the cracked old patent-leather valise she had had when she came to this house a bride. She did not believe it had been off the place since then. Facing the house, she saw it truly: falling-down, paint-peeling, ugly and poor. She thought of Jake inside, sitting at the kitchen table where she had told him to wait some hours ago; she had forgotten all about it. She thought of Jud walking off with all his wits and his strength and his youth about him, and she said to herself, I reckon Jake and me and the house are kind of piti-ful-looking.

When she entered the house it seemed quieter and emptier than usual, just knowing that Jud would not be back. He had closed the door to his room. Habit, she guessed, passing it. She could not look into it yet. She went to the kitchen and spoke gently to Jake, telling him he could move, and said, "We're alone now, Jake. There's just the two of us."

And she gave him a large slice of strawberry-iced cake, though it was just before his supper.

About dusk she went to Jud's room. It's emptiness gave her the feeling he was dead, too. And she felt guilty at the lack of emotion she felt at the thought. She took down the black-and-white pictures one by one, running over in her mind the idea of taking in a boarder. But who was there to board in Marigold? she wondered. The pretty young schoolteachers all boarded at Homer Brown's, by custom. Besides, she knew they would not want to stay where Jake was.

She made piles of things to throw away and put everything she was going to keep from the various drawers into one drawer. She had swept half the room when she saw Brother Moore pass by one of the low windows on his way around to the front of the house. She put down the broom and looked at herself in the bureau mirror. She buttoned the neck of her blouse and ran her fingers about her hair. By the time she came into the hall, Brother Moore had entered the front door and was coming down the hall calling, "Mrs. Darby. It's Brother Moore calling."

They met just outside Jud's door and shook

hands. "I thought you weren't to church Sunday," he said. "Then I saw you sitting way over on the right side 'stead of the left. Behind Miss Loma's big green hat. I declare I could hardly see you. Then I said to myself, I haven't seen Jud here for . . ."

At the moment, he saw over her head just as she reached behind her to close the door.

"He's gone?" he said, incredulously. "Has he really gone?"

"Yes," she said. "Jud has gone. And I was just thinking it's like he's dead. But that time comes to us all, don't it, Brother Moore? When our grown children leave us. Even if they just get married, they ain't ours any longer."

Brother Moore shrugged, and his limp pale hand circumscribed nothingness. "But, Mrs. Darby," he said, and bit his lip.

For the last time Jud was quite close to her; she remembered the day he was born and in one instant, it seemed, his whole babyhood and boyhood too. She felt him in her arms again as if he were actually there, a baby. As if it were an actual physical occurrence, she felt her arms broken apart and with a sharp ache in her breast she felt him gone. She remembered a headful of shining golden curls and a tiny wet, pink mouth pursed to kiss her. Then, as if a great curtain had fallen across the past, all she saw and would remember forever was his great massive back walking away.

I wish he had said just Thank you, she thought. That's all children ever need say to their mommas and daddies; it's nice if they love you, but its all right if they don't. All you need is for them to appreciate the trouble you've gone to to bring them up; they ought to know what it's like—though they'll learn soon enough when they got kids of their own. They don't have to like where they were brought up or even how; but they ought just to appreciate getting there.

"What will you do?" Brother Moore said. "How can you do everything yourself? Even a young woman couldn't, Sister Darby."

"Oh, I got another son, Brother Moore, don't you remember?" she said.

She thought she wasn't going to think about the look on his face, and him a preacher of divine love and charity. She said, "Come and let's have a cup of tea."

She walked ahead, dusting her hands together, and he came behind; then suddenly they were running together; they had heard the commotion in the kitchen for the first time.

Jake was trying to restrain the hounds. They were jumping against the screen door. One had already burst the bottom part of the screen and started it ripping from the frame. Both were howling the long-lost wails of hounds. Before they reached them, the larger of the two had lunged through the screen and was free now with the other following him; skidding on their rear feet, they were around the side of the house and off down the road after Jud.

"Well, that's two less mouths to feed," she said wearily, and turned back to the kitchen to fix the tea.

She carried it into the dining room, and when they had drunk it Brother Moore clasped his hands on the table, closed his eyes, lowered his head and said, "Will you pray with me?"

When she had done so and he had gone, she went back into the kitchen. Jake was gone. For an instant, her heart pounding, she thought he had followed the others. Then she went onto the porch and he was sitting on the back steps staring off where the dogs had run, his knees hunched up close to him. She said from the doorway, softly, "Come in, Son."

He did not move and she thought, I never called him by any other name but his given one before. She said again, gently, "Son."

When he did not move this time, she thought, He's not use to it yet. I got to say it a lot so he'll get use to it. She called again, "Jake. Son. Come inside. It's getting to be suppertime."

He'll forget them, she thought. But it was as if Jake knew that too and did not want to. He took one last long lingering look before he came inside.

And she was not sure whether he ever had forgotten. She stared off toward the pasture now, where he had gone, wondering.

3

She was dead. He knew it was death. She did not move for a very long time while he watched, and then he knew it was death. He had loved animals and they had been taken from him, but only after he had watched a long time and they had stayed still. And she was that still, like everywhere after a summer storm. He sat, and in the way that was his, after a time he said, "Ma. . . ."

She did not answer. She had not answered him all morning. When he opened his eyes to daytime, for the first time in the forty years of his life he had not heard her in the house. He knew it was home. The window was by the bed, and above his head was where the rain had come and spread long brown streaks that dried and peeled.

He got out of bed and went along the long hall, his feet cool on the bare floor, until he came to the room that was hers. He sat down watching; then it was two days, and he was tired. He got up, thinking how the cat ate mice that died and the dog went under the house with snakes; a cow down by the pond had stayed until there was nothing left but bones the buzzards had left.

He went outdoors, aware of the long, hot grass reaching after his legs as he crossed the yard. The chickens ran at him angrily, flew up at his knees and pecked the rounded toes of his worn-out brogans. He looked up at the sun, went inside the feed house and after a while came out with the right gunny sack. He stood, a tall thin figure against the sunlight, still except for the swinging arc of his arm spreading the feed about him. When it was done, he put the sack back exactly right and went on down to the back of the yard. He picked up a chick that came running in a great fright from inside the little shed when he opened the door. He held its soft yellow roundness close to him, sitting on the hole that pinched his bottom. And he tried to tell the animal in great dry sobs, but he knew no words for loss.

Finally he was crying for her. He came out blowing his nose on his sleeve and he set the chick down; still stooping, he watched as it ran toward the feed, crazylike, on its little thin legs. Then going on, he began to remember what she had always told him, and he zipped up his overalls. He hesitated at the steps leading up to the porch and looked at the house. It seemed dark inside after the brightness behind him, and he sat down on the steps and began to pull at the long summer-smelling grass crowding around them. The blades were slick and green and broke open wetly as his nail pressed into them. He sat a long time pulling them one by one, pressing them open, and then laying them neatly in a pile alongside him. Birds quietly stole pecans from the heavy greenness of the tree just beyond the gate, and at that instant a thin brown-and-white hound appeared in the empty road from the depths of the orchard and trotted in a sidelong fashion toward the gate; working it open with his nose, the dog came on into the yard, sniffing. Having nosed the pile of grass blades, it sat back on its haunches watching, hot and dusty, its red tongue lolling sideways out of a space between his teeth. Presently the man rose and walked out again into the yard from which he had just come, his eyes fixed where they had been for some time, as if to move them would be to forget. He walked to where the two-days-hung sheets idled stiffly in the one breath of air that stirred. He fumbled about them for some time, but finally his fingers found their answer and he began to pull them gently from the line. Crumpling them between his two great hands, he carried them carefully toward the house and gained the porch and was entering the house itself when its silence stopped him. He offered the sheets and withdrew them; offered them again anyway while the enormous tears that were his kind came down his cheeks. Behind him the hound, which had not yet moved, rose at the sound that spoke to it and, ambling to the man's heels, sat again on its haunches and, lifting its head, began a similar sound.

Then he turned for the first time, seeming to notice the dog, and looking down at it, was silent. The dog hushed too; it looked up eagerly, its drooling mouth open again. And then he heard the rumblings of his own stomach.

He stood a long time not knowing what to do. In his whole life he had never fixed food. Shortly, as if led by something unseen, he went the length of the house and entered the kitchen, with the dog just after him.

Someone had been there recently. Two places were laid opposite each other on the small oilcloth-covered table. The cover to a jar of grape jelly had slipped askew and black ants filled the empty half. He smelled oilcloth and crackers stored against wetness in an old wooden cabinet propped against the far wall. He went to it and opened the doors; then the smell of confined bread was even stronger. He saw cold biscuits and corn bread wedges on a chipped white plate, and he took the plate down, already crowding food into his mouth. The dog whined and he threw it a biscuit; the dog gulped it whole, then twitched its behind, whining again. He threw it the last corn bread and watched as the dog wolfed it, scattering crumbs in all directions. He stood, waiting, listening; in the silence, he heard a fly buzz. Presently something led him to the other side of the house to the screened porch. He lowered a bucket into the cistern and brought up water and they both drank from the dipper.

Sometime in the late afternoon, after he had gone many times into her room and looked at her and come out again and walked around the house and returned again and repeated the whole process, he found himself going down the road on his way to town. At each bend in the road he turned back, his face screwed up as he faced the sun's setting, his arm raised and gesturing, his throat convulsive, and the empty countryside filled with all the sounds he could utter: telling her he was going for help. Then, going on, he stopped again, each time uttering the sounds again, but sometimes gently, and with a meaning so different the sounds themselves sounded different; stooping, holding out his hand, trying to snap his fingers, calling the dog that had fled with a great yelp after the first time it had entered her room with him and sniffed around the bed.

The sun had gone by the time he entered town, but there were several hours of daylight left yet. The sun's passing made the day a little cooler and the shirt stuck wetly to his back began to dry as he gained the wooden sidewalks of the town and with a high loping step picked his way between the broken planks.

"Here he comes," called someone from the porch of the first store.

48

"Where you been, Jake?" called somebody else sitting in the circle of cane-bottomed chairs.

As he came up to the little store, another man said, "You been up to Memphis going to town, Jake?" and everybody laughed.

The first man shot a long brown stream of tobacco over his stomach and into the grass. "Naw," he said, "I bet he's been up to Washington, D. C., helping out there, hey, Jake?" and everybody laughed so hard Cotter May had a terrible fit of coughing.

The mute stood shaking his head, saying the sound that was *n*.

"He says naw," somebody said, and somebody else said, "Well, where you been at, Jake?"

He hung his head and went on. Somebody called after him, "You ain't crazy, are you, Jake?" and somebody else called the answer, "Naw, but you ain't far from it are you, Jake?" And this time the laughter was drowned out by the sound of flying gravel as a car from the country tore through town too fast.

He was alone until he crossed the side road and came to the next store. Nothing but a hound was on the porch. He tried to step over it, but miscalculated distance as he often did and stepped on its tail. He felt a great rush of pity, but at the dog's yowling someone opened the screen door into him and he forgot the dog.

"Oh, it's just a houn'," the woman said, and

stepped aside. "How you, Jake?" she said as he came in; then, shifting a large sack of groceries, she started for the door; but he brushed at her arm, afraid to touch it, remembering not to touch anyone; tears came with his effort and when he opened his mouth, nothing came out except saliva.

"Ooo, I declare to my soul," the woman said, turning away. She was quite large, going down the walk in a dress patterned all over with large purple poppies. He felt dizzy watching the design in motion as she walked away. Someone spoke to him from behind the counter, a face kind and familiar. "Jake, do you want to go to the bathroom? It's right back there through that door." He stood just inside the store shaking his head, trying to seek control over crying. The tears welled in his eyes as he stood blinking; finally they welled over.

"You take him, Thomas," the woman said. A little Negro boy seated on a pile of feed sacks stared at her openmouthed and said, "Naw sir, Miss Loma, he liable to have warts."

"Oh, get on out of here," she said, and the little boy picked up a bottle of orange pop and fled. Taking Jake's elbow, she propelled him to his duty. He performed it. When he returned, she scanned to see that he had closed his fly.

"You wanna banana caramel, Jake?" she said, reaching into the mottled case. He shook his head. Her hand moved from one box of candy to another, touching them lightly. "Candy ice cream cone?

50

Sour ball? Baseball sucker? Not licorice," she said, turning up her nose. He shook his head each time. "Sure you do," she said, and her hand returned to the caramels, deciding for him. She took one of the hard yellow squares from the case and put it into his hand. He stood looking down at it. "Here," she said, and took it and removed the slick waxed paper. Then she put it into his hand again, and as soon as he smelled its sweetness, saliva formed in his mouth and he felt hunger pains in his stomach. He put it into his mouth. Two men stopped a small tractor outside the door and came inside with a heavy clumping of boots and a terrible smell of sweat. They took Cokes out of the ice case and settled down into chairs. Miss Loma leaned over the counter and talked to them, stopping several times for children who came for popsicles, or for ladies who had forgotten several little things when they shopped in the morning, or who just wanted a cold Coke. Jake stood at his spot. If someone spoke to him, he rolled his eyes in their direction. The candy was a large unmelting hump in his cheek. Once a little boy howled, "You got mumps, Jake!" and the little girl with him ran screaming into the road.

"If he weren't the preacher's boy, I declare to my soul, I don't know what all I wouldn't do to that child," Miss Loma said, and shook her head. She picked up the empty bottles the men had left and put them into the Coke case. "Where's your Ma, Jake?" she said. "She didn't shop Monday."

His eyes and mouth opened in a round surprised manner, the candy fell from inside his cheek into the center of his mouth, and his teeth fell shut over it. Suddenly the sweetness began to flow down his throat, and pressed against the roof of his mouth, the caramel began to melt—it was suddenly soft-feeling, and he touched it experimentally with his tongue.

"Good?" Miss Loma said. "Want another?" But she was busy straightening up at that moment and did not get it.

He knew that there was something besides the candy; it had been just within reach and now hung just out of it. As best he could, he searched for it. But he could not push aside the taste, the smell, the feel of the candy, and he could know fully only one thing at a time. Miss Loma was leading him to the door now, telling him it was time for him to go home, time to close the store. He suddenly stood on the porch and watched the door closed in his face. The candy was still too large for him to speak. Miss Loma stood inside motioning him down the road, her face a round white circle against the dark interior.

He turned finally. A few pink tinges remained in the sky, but for the most part it was rain-gray. He walked in the twilight through the almost empty town. Miss Alma, the postmistress, was rocking on her front porch and said, "Evenin', Jake." Behind her, her lamp was a warm yellow spot in the grow-

52

ing dark. Crickets in the deep grass along the roadside began to sound. Ahead, a man was pumping water for his horse in a little shed set in the center of town; the clang of the iron pump was loud in the supper-hour quiet, as was even the rush of water and the sound of the horse's drinking. "Evenin', Jake," the man said and doffed his hat. "How's your Ma?" And he turned back to the horse, expecting no answer. He did not even see Jake stop and stand and look. He got on his horse and rode away in the opposite direction, leaving behind a cloud of dust that filtered through Jake's nostrils, seeped even through his lips closed tightly over the candy, flavoring it with dust and grit, and hurt in his eyes, until the postmistress called gently through the near dark, "Get out of the dust, Jake."

Then he moved, his gaunt figure continuing in its funny high loping step down the middle of the road. He turned off the main road and down the side one that he would follow to its very end. He passed all the houses and went for some time along the road that narrowed until it was hardly big enough for one car; on each side was a narrow ditch, weed-filled, and beyond them nothing but gullies and pasture land; occasionally he smelled wild plum and honeysuckle and once the tickling, pepperish smell of tiny wild roses; but mostly he smelled the stink of ragweed and simply the heavy grassy smell of summer. His shoes hurt him and a rock had bruised an instep through one thin sole. He was feeling the pain of it when suddenly he gave a little choking sound and with a last flood of sweetness the candy slipped down the back of his throat and left his mouth, at last, free. For a while he could think only of that and went over and over the surprise of losing the candy. But then he suddenly sat down on the side of the road and, with his head hung down between his knees, moaned over and over all that he had wanted to say. Spent at last, he got up and continued on the road until he came up against the gate. He stood outside and looked at the dark house. It was the first time in his life there had been no one to meet him and no lamp lit. When he had passed through the gate he went forward hesitantly, his mouth hung open, his hands groping toward the side of the house, though dark had not yet come full. He entered, closing the door softly behind him, and faced down the long dark hall expecting still that someone would come into it. He went its length and reached the kitchen and saw it still as he had quit it a long time ago. He went into all the rooms of the house, hers among them, and looked at her without surprise, and continued to look about the house, still expecting someone. At last he did not know what to do with himself, though he knew the ritual that should be followed. He went finally and got into bed, all her warnings clear in his head. He looked once toward the lamp, but he did not touch it.

The next morning he found milk and bread and

butter. He went out across the yard to the hen house and carried in eggs in a worn enamel pan, but once inside, he put them in the center of the table, not knowing what else to do with them. He was sitting at the kitchen table, still in the clothes he had slept in, very carefully using a knife to put butter on his bread, when he heard a truck stop. He put all the bread in his mouth and sat very quietly, chewing. He heard the car door slam, and presently he heard the scrape of the screen door being pulled open across the floor; then he heard heavy footsteps. He was hidden by the door when someone came into the room next to him—the dining room, where the icebox was kept. He could see slightly between the doorframe and the door as the big colored man struggled to lift the fifty pounds of ice into the box. Then he slung the tongs over his shoulder and called, "Missus, it's Preacher with the ice."

In the silence afterward, Jake could hear the man's heavy breathing. He knew who the man was and why he was there. He knew that now it was going to be all right. Presently, the man moved to the door of the bedroom and called, "Hello, Missus."

Jake could hear the alarm clock ticking in there. Then he could hear the heavy steps of the man going away, and his voice, fainter, calling, "It's Preacher."

Then the man was on the front porch. He heard the door slam behind him. And he knew how it would look: the empty porch, the stilled swing, ahead the empty road and quiet flat land; and the field, still too, rising in the distance to a road where you could see the white steeple of the church. He thought he heard a bird sing, and he could feel the warmth of the day flush on his face as he knew the man could; sweat stood out on his forehead. Presently he heard the man open the front door to re-enter the house, and he stood up and went down the hall, meaning neither to be quiet nor to make noise, but the man did not hear him. He was in her room, bending over the bed. Jake stood outside the door, watching. He heard the man's heavy intake of breath, watched as he held her arm a moment, then let it fall quickly. He drew the sheet up over her face. He came into the hall and followed it to the kitchen. Jake was seated again at the table, a piece of bread halfway to his mouth. He looked up at the man without sound or expression, and the man gazed back at him silently. Once he opened his mouth as if to say something, but then he closed it and his head gave a little shake. He leaned against the doorframe and wiped his face with a handker-chief; then he sort of half blew his nose and shook his head again and went on out the back door. Jake heard the flutter and squawking of chickens and heard the man spreading their feed. For a while he heard nothing, then the man's voice farther away calling, "*Su pig pig pig,*" and the sound of corncobs falling into their trough. In a little while he came back up the short hill, puffing from the climb, and passed the back door and said, "No time now for a cow." He stood at the bottom of the back steps and called up, "You stay there. You stay there. You hear, Mister Jake?"

He buttered a slice of bread and put it into his mouth. It was then, while he was chewing, he knew that sometime before he had heard the truck drive away. He got up and went down the hall and took the sheet away from her face. Then he returned to his seat in the kitchen.

When the first ones to hear the news came, he was still sitting there: still eating the loaf of bread and the hand-shaped mound of white butter.

"You eat that whole loaf up, Jake?" said one of the ladies.

When he looked up, there was a whole brood of them looking at him from a semicircle; their brightness almost frightened him. They wore flowered dresses and colored glass beads; their cheeks were red spots and their mouths narrow red lines; their faces were freshly powdered, and some were the color of flour while others were like peaches in bloom. One lady, with bracelets that slid down her arm when she reached out, took the bread away from him, though he was still hungry.

"Oh, the poor *thing*," said another. "Do you think he knows?"

57

"Bound to," said another. "He's bound to've looked into her room. They say it's been several days."

"But I mean, do you think he *understands?*" said the other.

They were all silent, looking at him. Finally one said, "Come on out on the porch, Jake, and get some fresh air."

He got up and followed her. The others came behind. "We could take his mind off it," said one, "if only we knew whether it was *on* it or not." She looked back at the near-empty polka-dotted bread wrapper.

Miss Hattie McGaha, a thin little birdlike lady, said, "Well, there's no sense fixing him something to eat," and she followed the others, fluttering her hands helplessly.

From the porch he could see others coming, clouds of dust preceding and following the various cars, horses, trucks; some came on foot at a half-run, shielding their faces as vehicles passed them and arriving covered with a gold-colored film. They came through the gate, subdued, and greeted one another on the porch in quiet tones. Jake sat in a rocking chair in the midst of them, staring out at the front yard. Everyone looked at him but no one spoke except two or three men in shirtsleeves who patted him on the back and said, "It's okay, boy. It's okay."

The ladies stood off together in a little cluster, just

not knowing this time what to do at all.

Whenever there had been a death, he had gone too; now it had come home to him; the people were coming here. Brother Patrick came, wearing a suit even though it was summertime. People stepped aside as he came up and shook Jake's hand, the way he would have done with anyone. Then he opened his mouth as if he wanted to say something, but nothing seemed to come, so he closed it and just shook harder. Someone whispered in his ear, "She's inside, Brother." Then he let go and went into the house.

Things moved on through the afternoon like that. People were all over the porch and the yard, in groups now, talking louder, laughing if they wanted. Once someone brought him a glass of iced tea, and once someone brought him a bowl of homemade ice cream. It was then a long car came down the road and pulled around to the side of the house. By the time he finished the ice cream, it had gone slowly away, and a man near him remarked that it was a re- lief to get that done. Someone touched him on the shoulder to go to the bathroom, and when he passed through the kitchen he saw more cakes and pies on the table than he had ever seen all together before. He sat on the porch again later, thinking of them. The sound of talking went on around and above him, rising and falling like bee hums; he rocked with the rhythm, warm air falling over him and falling away again, the smells of grass and clover so intense, he knew how it would feel to have his face in them.

For a while all he knew after that was the far-off hum of speech and the sweet smell of clover; and after that, for a long time, all he knew was the look of the black car going away.

When he woke, he saw a group of people standing at the gate, shaking hands all around. Carrying cakes and pies, everyone left but two men. The one he knew best, Wilroy Sheaffer, said, "He's awake," as they came back across the porch.

The other, Cotter May, said, "You want some supper, Jake?"

There were still a few people in the yard, and he could hear someone in the house. The day had lessened, and with it the heat. He stretched his legs out and rocked a little bit, and then he nodded. Just as the two men were turning away, Jake got up suddenly and caught Wilroy by the sleeve. He told him and told him about the chickens, pointing at the hen house until finally Wilroy understood. "You hear that, Cotter," he said. "He knows it's time to feed them chickens. It's been done, Jake," he said. "It's all done been taken care of. Everything." He called into the kitchen to his wife, who had been a friend of Jake's mother, "Mary Margaret! Woman, fix this boy some supper."

When his wife came from the kitchen, he said, "Do you know this boy knew it was time to feed them chickens?"

Mary Margaret beamed at Jake. "Well, now, I declare. Your supper's on the table, Jake. *Table*," she said, raising her voice and her finger to point at the same time.

Everybody watched him as he went inside. "That *boy* is near 'bout old as I am," Cotter said from the swing.

"Oh well, you know," Mary Margaret said, in a hushing tone.

Cotter's spinster sister, Ruth Edna, who had been closer to Jake and his mother than anyone, had come onto the porch from the kitchen now. She gave Cotter a swat on the head with one of the cardboard fans the undertaker had left. "Now we don't know how much *he does know*," she said.

Mary Margaret said, "We ought to go in and see about him. We're the ones to, now."

"Well, then we got to get on home," Wilroy said.

They all went down the hall, single file. "I hate to think of all we got to do when we get there," Mary Margaret said.

The Mays lived together, and Ruth Edna looked over her shoulder at her brother. "Us too," she said meaningfully.

"Now I don't no'm," Cotter said, grimacing. He rubbed his hand across his back. "This day has been about all I can take. I'm wore out." He coughed lightly, ignoring the thin set of his sister's lips.

Jake was seated at the table carefully picking the lima beans out of his bowl of succotash: popping them into his mouth and sucking his fingers loudly. They all huddled around him making little sounds, offering a spoon and tucking a napkin under his chin. Finally they decided to leave him alone. "Let be what'll be," was the way Wilroy put it; and they were all anxious to get home.

The last stragglers, who had been on a little inspection tour of the house and yard, came around to the back of the house just then and yelled up that they were going. "Wait a minute," Mary Margaret said. "Did you all bring the chocolate cake or the banana pudding?"

"Pudding and a little pan of fudge," came back the answer. "Eloise says leave that."

Mary Margaret carried them out onto the porch. "No sense leaving them here for him to get sick on eating them all up at once."

She came back into the house and when her somewhat broad expanse had cleared the doorway, Jake saw the two being carried away as the others had been. The little tin pan of fudge caught a last glint of afternoon sun and shone for a second like silver. The succotash was tasteless in his mouth tuned for sweetness. The two women, who had looked around their dead friend's house to see that everything was all right, came back now, bustling themselves together, ready to go. "Well, boy," Wilroy said.

"Well," Mary Margaret said.

"There's milk in the box," Ruth Edna said. "*Milk.*"

62

"I hate to leave him," Mary Margaret said. "Dark coming on. You think he knows how to light the lamp?"

"Sure," Wilroy said. "He knew about them chickens, didn't he? Don't forget to feed the chickens tomorrow now, boy," he said, louder. "And if you don't know what to do with that cow, put a rope around her neck and bring her into town. Somebody'll help you."

"He can't understand all that," his wife said.

"Shoot," Wilroy said, as if somebody were deaf, "that boy can understand more'n we think he can. Come on. We got to get home, woman."

The women stood at the table, looking down at the last two cakes. Between them, Jake looked up at them and then down at the cakes. "You reckon we ought to leave one?" Mary Margaret said.

"Oh, I reckon one," Miss May said. "It seems so funny giving all those others back like that."

"Well, we couldn't have left them here for him to eat all up at once," Mary Margaret said.

"No," said the other. "And wasn't there a lot! Wouldn't she have been proud?"

"Bless her heart," Mary Margaret said. "Do you want to leave yours or mine?"

"Oh, I don't know," Ruth Edna said. They studied the two. "Mine's not much. Just something I did up as quick as I could when I heard. Fell a little. Didn't give it good time to cool."

Mary Margaret put her head on one side. "Hmn,

a little," she said. "Not your best." They looked at hers: angel food with a perfect rise, and sworls of white icing lapping each other all over it: all the ladies had exclaimed. "I did put a little into mine," she said. "I tell you. I could take mine on up to the cake sale at the Baptist church tomorrow."

"Well, go ahead," Ruth Edna said. "Mine's littler anyway. Here, Jake. Here, honey. Eat this nice cake." She cut him a piece and put it on the side of his plate. "I'm going to put the rest up here," she said, and put it in the top part of the cupboard.

"He's watching," Mary Margaret said.

"Well," Miss May said, hesitantly. "Oh come on, they're blowing the horn."

Mary Margaret took her cake and followed her out of the room; then she suddenly came running back in and said, "Bye-bye, Jake, honey. Bye-bye. You come uptown soon now, you hear."

It was going to be evening. There was quiet in the chicken yard and quiet out over the garden. Beyond it, dark had come into the gullies, and a row of little wild persimmon trees stood out black on the horizon. He could see all the way across to them from where he sat in the kitchen, and two birds, black as ravens against the red-and-gold sky, hovered over them an instant, then settled out of sight. In the silence of outdoors, he heard a walnut fall from the old tree in the side yard and break open against the hard ground. And in the silence of the house he heard only the clock in the bedroom and the sound of his own breathing. He was alone and he knew that.

Presently he ate the cake. His fingers dug into and out of the dark sticky chocolate, and he sucked them loudly, glad of his own noise. He had no hunger for more when he finished the piece and did not move from the table. He could feel that beyond him the house was dark, knew that, sitting in the doorway, he was watching the last of daylight. Occasionally, from a good distance away, he would catch the sound of a car horn. He thought of the dog and wished that it had not left him. He remembered the whole afternoon and was glad of the noise and the people as they had moved about him. He wished they had not gone away.

When the kitchen had grown dark, he moved his chair out onto the old lean-to porch where there was still light enough to see a little ahead of himself. His hands hung down empty and still between his knees, and he wondered if it was time for him to go to bed.

A flashlight suddenly shone on and off at the bottom of the steps like a giant mosquito. Then a voice said through the dark, "It's Jurldeane, Mister Jake." He heard her approach, and presently she was right by him and had turned the flashlight on underneath her chin. "See," she said. "Jurldeane. Your momma's wash girl."

She flashed the light around inside the kitchen. He watched it bounce ball-like from one wall to another; then it lit on the lamp. "Come on inside, Mister Jake, and let's get us some light," she said. He followed her and stood quietly while she lit it. In the dark he could smell on her clothes Clorox and a clean starchy smell; when she moved he smelled her body, warm with the effort of her walk; then, with the sudden yellow light making dark hollows in her face as she bent over to turn up the wick, he smelled kerosene. "You eat supper, I see," she said, looking down at his used dishes. He followed her glance and looked down at them too. Then when she raised her eyes, he raised his and they looked at each other across the lamplight. "I knew they wouldn't be here now," she said. Her full bottom lip, opening, was shiny with snuff. "Here you are. Here I am. Where are they?" she said. "Leaving you all alone the first night they took her away." Her mouth closed with a clamp, and she sat down heavily in the rickety kitchen chair. "Po' thing," she said, watching his face as he sat down opposite. Suddenly she leaned out and brought his plate across the table toward her. "What's this? Choc'late cake? Whose, you reckon?" She licked her finger, then slid it across the plate where the cake had been and licked it again. "Not Miss Mary Margaret's." She considered, running her tongue all around her lips. "Don't recognize that," she said, finally. "Is they mo'?"

He followed her arm as it motioned the plate about. "Mo'?" she said.

The plate rested on the table again and she tapped it with a large forefinger. "Cake?" He looked up and met the eyes that asked him something. The woman looked back at him for some seconds, her head cocked to one side. "Hmm-um," she said, finally. "Po' thing," and put her hands on the table and pushed herself up. She looked behind the old curtain covering the shelves on one side of the room and then crossed over to the cupboard and opened that. She turned grinning at him, the cake plate in her hand. "Here it is," she said, coming back to the table. "We going to have us some cake eatin' now, Mister Jake. It going to be me and you." She pushed his plate back to him and set one down in front of herself. She cut two large pieces and placed one on each plate; then she broke off a piece of hers with her fingers and ate it. Her tongue curled around each fingertip afterward, licking it. Jake watched, and when she said, "Eat that cake up," he began to eat. She smiled at him when he licked his fingers, and he opened his mouth wide showing his teeth. Once she stopped chewing and said, "Huh, oleo," and then began to chew again. Jake finished first, and she cut him a thin sliver to eat on while she finished. He did not understand at first, and the woman said again, "Go 'head." He ate, and when they had both finished, she put slices on their plates again. She got up once and went into the next room; he sat without chewing, thinking she had gone; then she reappeared, a pitcher of milk in her hand, and poured them glasses full. They sat back in their chairs, alternately eating and licking and drinking, with no other light in the house, and no other sound save that of the clock. Her face was shining and dark in the pale light, and he did not once take his eyes from it. Whenever she looked at him, she smiled or refilled his glass or his plate. She caught a lightning bug in her hand, then released it for him to see; they watched it flicker away into the dark of the house beyond them. "No noise. No light. Nuthin'," Jurldeane said. She was quiet a moment, listening. Jake stopped chewing, watching her. "I use to pass by on the road upside this house some evenin's," she said. He watched as a sweat bead slid from her forehead down the side of her face, watched as she leaned over and lowered the wick of the lamp. "And we would wonder what goes on inside that house when night comes. What does he do. It always so quiet, so still like. Only sometime we see your momma passing up and down before the light, going from one room to another. Never did see you, Mister Jake. We would wonder—do he go to bed soon as dark comes, or do he set around and make some kind of talk with his momma so she have some company?" She was quiet a moment, thinking back; then she looked up at him, her eyes wide and wet. "Now I know," she said. "Now I know."

She sat back, her arms crossed beneath her breasts. "We all got some kind of cross to bear," she said. "Your momma had hers. But what I don't see, though the Lord has His ways, is who else going to take it up now."

By the low light of the lamp her eyes looked deep in their bright, white sockets. He watched them, listening to the soft singsong of her voice. And suddenly she was saying, "Oh Lord, hush now. Hush, Lamb of God."

She came around the table and pressed his head against her skirt. Once again, and for the last time, he had the warm body smell of a woman's lap for his head.

She held him until he was spent, murmuring, "Po' thing, po' old man child," and finally lifted his head and said, "Now blow your nose." And he took the paper napkin she handed him and tried to do it.

"I don't know what you going to do, Mister Jake, I declare to my soul I don't." She stood looking down into the lamp as if it might hold an answer. Then she looked at him and said, "You know how to light this thing? Turn it down and blow it out?" He looked at her eagerly, silently, his mouth hung open. "You don't any more know what I'm talking 'bout than the cat flies," she said. "Here." From the curtained shelves she took a box of old candle ends, lit one and let it drip into a saucer. Then she secured the candle in the hot tallow and put it on the table before him. "You know how to blow that out?" she said. He leaned forward and did it with a little puff of spit. "Now I'm going to light it again," she said, "and when you get into bed, you be sure and blow it out, you hear? Can you nod your head if you hear?" He did that.

"I got to go now," she said. "It's on about nine o'clock." She collected the dishes from the table and rinsed them in a bucket of water sitting in the sink, then laid them on the drainboard. "Eat from these tomorrow," she said. She looked back at him, feeling that his eyes had never left her.

"I declare to my soul I don't," she said. She picked up her flashlight and tested it. His eyes blinked with the on-and-off of the light. Then she came across the room and began turning down the wick bit by bit. But suddenly she stopped when it was almost out. They were still, looking at each other, their faces shadowed with the wick's final fluttering. "I don't want to," she said, "but I got to." Then she blew out the wick, and they were alone by the thin light of the candle.

He knew that now she was going.

She stood in the doorway and looked back at him. "Get into bed now," she said. "Blow out that candle."

He made no movement, no sign. His arms lay along the table encircling the empty plate, his hands were still. Suddenly the leg bent up under his chair gave an involuntary jerk and straightened out before him with a scrape of his heel. He jumped and ran his thumb under his overall strap, pulling it back up on his shoulder. He stared straight ahead of himself for a while. Then he put his fingers in his plate and slowly began to eat again.

"Something will happen," she said, quietly. "Something will happen, Mister Jake." She stood hesitantly, weighing the flashlight in her hand. "And I tell you," she said, "I will be over myself to see to yo' wash."

She looked once over her shoulder at the dark, at the direction in which she would go. The sky was lightened a moment by heat and she saw off as far as the persimmon trees. There was no sound in all of the countryside and then she heard him. The sound evoked a rush of her own tears, and she gasped to keep them back for now. She almost went, but then she took one more look at the thin, straightened legs in their dirty, creased overalls, and at the bent shoulders in the once starched shirt so carefully turned at the collar, and she came back into the room. She stood just behind him—in all instinct yearning to touch him again. But this time she did not. She bent low toward his back and whispered in a voice just before sobbing, "It ain't right. I know that. The Lord knows it too. And if I didn't know folks, Mister Jake, I'd stay. I would."

Then she was gone.

It was a little while and then he was quiet. He picked up the napkin again and made a stab at his nose. Then he went to bed. Then he got up and came back into the room and blew out the candle. Then he went back to bed again, stumbling in the dark.

In the morning there was bread and butter and milk again. He ate it. Afterward, he put the dishes in the bucket of water, pulled them out again, and put them on the drainboard. In a little while he went out across the yard to the bathroom and on his way back to the house, he fed the chickens. He was standing in the bedroom, looking down at the dirt covering his pants, when someone came into the room behind him. When he turned around, the man said, "How do, Jake. Earl Metcalf. We uptown decided the thing to do was me to take that cow over to my barn and bring you milk every evenin'. You just ain't going to be able to take care of no cow." Then he saw the man go out to the barn and presently walk away, waving the cow before him.

It was when he had gotten hungry again and eaten all the jelly and crackers that he noticed the dirt again. After a bit, he suddenly sat down and got all his clothes off. Two buttons fell off his shirt onto the floor. He got down on his knees and put his finger on one and pushed it around awhile; then he was finally able to curl it up under his fingertip and slip it into the palm of his hand. He did that with the other one and wadded his shirt up with the buttons inside it. He found clothes like those he had taken off and he got them on, except for his shirt-tail, which trailed out. Then he started uptown, the wadded-up shirt carefully beneath his arm. He walked slowly at first, but by the time he entered town he had again hit his high, loping stride. When someone spoke to him, he made some sort of sound in return, opened his mouth wide and grinned.

When he entered the store, the woman said, "We were talking 'bout you just now, Jake. Come on in." Someone near the Coke case handed him a cold bottle. "I got a boy that's going to bring you down some groceries every week for fifteen cents," Miss Loma said. "Then I'll send a little bill up to the bank in Senatobia every week, and they'll pay me out of the little money your momma left."

"He don't understand all that talk," said a man sucking on a toothpick.

"I know it," the woman said. "But I feel like I ought to speak it out in public in case there's ever any question about the money. You know how the government is."

"That's right," said another lady. She handed Jake a package of Nabs. "And somebody will be taking him a little cooked something now and then. I declare, look at him. He's got on clean clothes and looks almost decent as she kept him."

"What's that—a shirt? What's he want?" said the man, wiggling his toothpick to the other side.

He offered it again; this time the woman noticed it. "You reckon he wants it washed?" Miss Loma said. She took it and opened it, and the buttons fell on the floor. He began to nod his head. "Look, you reckon it's the buttons?" she said. She picked them up and said, "You want the buttons back on, Jake?" She looked at the others. "Yes, I believe that's what

73

he wants. I'll do 'em and wash it," she said. "You come back for it in a few days."

"Now, can you beat that?" the other lady said. "Jake, you got any more sewing, you bring it in. We in the Baptist Thursday Club can all take turns doing it."

One by one those who came to the store left again. He sat for a long time on a nail keg near the door. He ate what was given to him and grinned at those who spoke to him. Occasionally someone would say, "You ain't crazy, are you, Jake? But you ain't far from it!" and then they would slap him on the back, and he would grin very wide at them. They would say then, "You're all right, boy!"

Miss Loma said, "Closing time, Jake. Early on Wednesdays." He went out the screen door when she held it open. There was hardly anyone in town when he walked through, but those who were there all spoke to him. The filling station was still open, but the last car drove away as he passed by, and the owner disappeared into his house next door. A chicken ran ahead of him in the middle of the road, and he *whoosed* at it; from out of sight someone called, "You git him, Jake."

Then he was turning off the main road and going down the road that led past all houses and on into the silence of the countryside and finally to his own gate. He came up to it and looked ahead at the quiet house. When he entered it, no one was there. No one came all afternoon. When the chickens began to make a racket in the yard, he went out and fed them and then he came in and ate on the baloney and the bread Miss Loma had given him. He found a little pail of milk on the table, and he drank that.

It was not long before he noticed the day had lessened; the sun had spread out into long, runny streaks of red and gold, and the persimmon trees begun to darken against the horizon. He took his chair out onto the lean-to and propped in it up against the house, his feet hooked into the rungs. He waited for dark, the candle already in his hand, the match laid carefully by. He knew how to give it one good strike and afterward stick it in the bucket of water. It was almost time to light it when he saw the birds again, hovering over the line of trees before they settled in them out of sight. In the garden the weeds had grown, and dark came early in the tall grass. Once he thought he saw movement there, and he leaned forward quietly looking—he thought it might be a dog—but he never saw anything again, and he settled back in his same position.

When it came full dark, he lit the candle and went indoors. He took off his clothes tonight and lay flat with a sheet up over him when the candle was out.

Usually he went to sleep quickly. Tonight he lay awake. He looked at his clothes lying in a heap on the floor in the moonlight and in the quiet and dark gradually understood, as much as he could, that no one was going to stay here again. He was completely alone.

He lay awake as the night and its silence deepened. He had always known silence, but suddenly he was afraid of it. He sat up, startled, and with one terrified, but reassuring cry, called out at the top of his lungs, telling them all, telling everybody, the one thing in the world he did know fully: that as deep as his own silence was, it was nowhere near so deep as hers.

4

Ruth Edna stood on the porch and watched
Jake go down the path to the gate. He
could manage her latch and lifted it, passed
out to the exact center of the road and tugging up
the straps of his overalls, went down the road and
out of sight. A rooster ran from the yard after him,
pecking frantically as if he had dropped something.

Ruth Edna glanced upward at clouds sun-tinged
and bright as gold, banked in a sky that would have
nothing to do with rain. She turned back to the
breezeway, reminding herself next time to see
about Jake's straps. Off the breezeway's other end
was the garden where only weeds flourished in the
dry ground, and goldenrod, the color of mustard,
rose in graceful spikes taller than the corn.

As she went along the breezeway, Cotter called
from his room, where he sat rocking, "What'd he
want?"

Otherwise she would not have stopped. "Sewing," she said. She held up denim work shirts so

worn they were almost white. Sleeves tangled in various ways held them together and suddenly, realizing Jake had been trying to make a bundle, she held them close. Then she smelled sweat, and more. The henhouse, she thought and knew she would wash the shirts too.

Cotter said, "All you do is sew for him. Why don't you sew for yourself. That dress you got on has a rip clear down the side."

"You tend to your own business. I'll tend to mine." Ruth Edna flung across the breezeway to her own room.

Large and dark, it served them as a dining room as well. All the furniture in the house had been her mother's, except a cedar chest Ruth Edna had managed to buy. Now she crossed over to it and lifted the lid. She put the shirts inside. On top lay a doll. When Ruth Edna took her out, her eyes, blue as blueing, flew open and stared. Ruth Edna kissed her mouth, a tea rose, pink and perfect. She ran her finger inside little curls coiled like springs and admired again the tiny patent-leather slippers; a thin strap across the instep buttoned onto a white pearl button no bigger than a raindrop. No one knew Ruth Edna had the doll, and she put her away again carefully. She put out a finger and closed her eyes. Not to would be like burying someone alive.

Afterward, she touched beneath her armpits with bath powder, changed her dress and was ready to go uptown when she heard a chirpy little voice down the breezeway: "Yoo-hoo. Ruth Ed—na!"

"In here," she called, knowing Hattie knew it. She pretended to look so she could peer into all the rooms.

When she had come in, Hattie stood transfixed. "Ruth Edna! Isn't that new?" Her eyes darted quickly about the room, at the unwashed dishes, at the unmade bed, at the scraps of Ruth Edna's dress still on the floor. To her surprise, she thought the kitchen floor had been mopped; then she saw it was just that something had been spilled—the sponge used to dab it up lay nearby.

Ruth Edna turned before the mirror. "It's not quite finished. The hem's just basted."

"I see." Hattie saw the thread coming out. "You going uptown? I am."

"Yes. Let's go."

They entered the breezeway and faced across an old apple orchard where the morning sun had just come to rest upon the tops of the squat, gnarled trees. Between the dark glistening leaves the apples hung light green, knotty and hard, and as sweet as they were ever going to get.

Looking about, Ruth Edna said, "I declare, it's going to be hot. I best get a towel."

She returned to the house, and Hattie crept down the breezeway. She had just gotten to Cotter's room when Ruth Edna came out another door and spoke right behind her: "He's there."

"Ruth Edna——!" Hattie's little hands flew to

her sparse breasts. Then breathless, she turned and bobbed up and down before Cotter's screen door trying to see inside his room. "Why! Is that you, Brother Cotter?"

"Oh, stop all that smirking up your face. He can't see out through that screen any better'n you can see in," Ruth Edna said.

"Why, Ruth Edna . . ." Hattie said.

"Don't pay no mind to her, Miss Hattie," Cotter said. "She ain't off right in the morning till she's had at somebody."

"Are we going uptown or not?" Ruth Edna said.

"Who's waiting for you there?" Cotter said. "Gary Cooper?"

"Now, you two," Hattie said. She was going to say goodbye, but suddenly with the condition Cotter was in, it seemed too final. She cried instead, "Keep alive . . . !" intending it to be cheery. Then realizing, she sank into herself horrified and fled the yard like a stray being chunked at.

Ruth Edna caught up with her at the gate. "I declare to my soul, Hattie McGaha. I always have thought your head was stuffed with fruitcake. Now I know it."

She wrapped her arms in the towel and folded them across her breasts, mummylike. She went ahead, and Hattie came along behind, a black umbrella opened over her head large as a parachute, covering her entirely except for her tottery legs beneath going along like a pair of old scissors, one barely slipping by the other.

From the wooden walk Ruth Edna could see their shadows chasing each other on the road below, wavery as water images. If Hattie hadn't carried that black mortuary-looking umbrella, they could have walked side by side instead of single file like this, looking like fools, she thought. She turned around and looked at Hattie hurrying along half out from under the umbrella, vulnerable as a turtle out of its shell, a smudge in the middle of her forehead. From Cotter's screen, she'd bet. She called, "Hattie, you got black soot all over your face."

"Oh, Ruth Edna!" Hattie cried; her mind jumped backward to who all they had seen, walking uptown. She lowered the umbrella and stood with the handle crooked over her arm like a parrot's beak, scrubbing at her face with a Kleenex till it fell into shreds.

Exasperated, Ruth Edna said, "Oh come on. You're not gettin' married today." She went ahead, thinking of a similar incident that happened once in a Memphis department store. She had a prissy little salesgirl who was annoyed because Ruth Edna didn't make up her mind. Finally she told the girl, "Honey, you got a big black smudge in the middle of your forehead."

"It's Ash Wednesday," the girl said.

That got the better of Ruth Edna. She slammed down the thread she had selected and left the store, boycotted it even through a sale on cotton dresses. Then, regretfully, she told Cotter the story.

"Stupid," he said. "That's something got to do with Catholics, not Lowenstein's Department Store."

Ruth Edna could remember now how she had stood, her mouth fallen open, wishing she could kick herself. Anybody in the world but a fool like her would have known that was some kind of foolishness nobody but a Catholic could think up.

"Hattie, you ever heard of Ash Wednesday?" she called.

"Ash *what!*" Hattie called, running forward.

"Oh, nothing," Ruth Edna said, satisfied.

When they entered Miss Loma's, Sadie Louise Murphy jumped from behind the door, like a scare for Halloween, and cried, "George Edwards is dead!"

"Oh my!" Hattie said.

"How'd that happen?" Ruth Edna said.

"He went out to the barn milking, and when he didn't come in, his wife went out and found him. He never even got started. The pail was dry as a bone and the cow bellowing. He'd just fallen over. Heart, they reckon."

"Did he fall in hay?" Hattie said. "I mean, not in a cow plop, did he? *Ooo.*"

"*Hat*—tie!" everybody said.

"Hattie, your head's stuffed just with nuts out of the fruitcake," Ruth Edna said, almost bitter.

She went off to the back of the store where the Coke machine was. Miss Loma was stacking cans of creamed corn and said, "Ruth Edna, you got Jake's sewing again this week?"

Ruth Edna dropped a dime in the machine. "Yes, why?"

"I just think it's my turn, is all," Miss Loma said, licking back a label. "But it seems like Jake hasn't learned to take it to nobody but you."

"That's because I've done it so much these past two months. I've got more time, not having a husband or kids or grandchildren like most folks, you know." Tears sprang to her eyes, and with a feeling of relief she let them stay; they might well be from drinking the fizzy cola too fast.

"Whew, I do," Miss Loma said. "It seems like I got to pee-pee on the run in the mornings to get all done in a day I got to do."

At that moment, from the front of the store, someone called, "We just seen Jake coming out of your house, Ruth Edna, when we come by."

"Jake?" Ruth Edna said. "I wonder why?"

"'Cause you got his sewing, I reckon," Miss Loma said.

"But he just brought it a while ago. I couldn't have done it yet."

"Well, he don't know that. Jake don't know the

morning from the evening."

"I reckon he knows that much," Ruth Edna said. She put her empty bottle into the rack like a honeycomb.

At the front of the store, Hattie, white as a sheet, stood and called, "Ruth Edna, I got to go."

"Go?" Ruth Edna came forward. "We just got here."

"I know, but I got to go. Listen, I'm in trouble. Bad trouble."

"Trouble?" everybody echoed, crowding around.

"I told you my bantam's sick. I've got the feeling something terrible has happened to him."

Without looking at one another, everyone agreed she ought to go home then. "Lord help us," Ruth Edna said, feeling helpless, and decided she might as well go too. She followed Hattie out of the store and said, "How do," generally to the men sitting on the porch: the Veazey brothers, Wilroy and several others she didn't look at long enough to recognize.

"How do, Miss Ruth Edna," they said in return, lifting hats. Having collected their mail on the way home to noon dinners, they had stopped to visit a while on Miss Loma's porch, and the air was sour with the smell of their sweat, soaked in black circles beneath their arms and in patches on their backs, except on Wilroy, who worked for a coal, ice and ginning company in Senatobia and wore a suit every day. The Veazeys had just come from their bottomland near where the government-built dam was going up. The possibilities of that, Lord! It was said the dam would run over into a spillway where there would be boating and fishing, swimming even! No one had ever dreamed of anything like that near Marigold. Ed Veazey squinted against the blue cigarette smoke in the air heavy as fog, hoisted his pants leg and applied coal oil Miss Loma had given him to his chigger bites. Blushing, Ruth Edna looked away from his hairy white legs; she had always thought Cotter the only one hiding such a sight under pants legs. Tell her men didn't have all the advantages in this world.

Hattie hurried away down the walk, the umbrella bobbing along like a cork floating, and Ruth Edna went after her at a half-run, forgetting her towel until she arrived breathless at Hattie's. Then she drew Hattie into the shade of the weeping willow, holding aside the branches like glass curtains of green crystals, the pointed leaves like little tongues flicking them with sharp edges as they passed. Hattie studied Ruth Edna's arms and swore in all honesty she did not see a single freckle. "Well, next time, wait," Ruth Edna said, her mouth drawn into a thin warning line.

"Ruth Edna," Hattie said, as they went on, "did you see Ed Veazey's legs?"

"Well, I didn't *look*, if that's what you mean. But I can tell you, men's legs are all the same."

"They are?" Hattie said, astonished.

"Men, Hattie," Ruth Edna said, sweeping her

85

arm protectively about her like a brooding hen, "have all the advantages in this world. They can hide their flaws, and they can marry if and when they choose." Her voice broke surprisingly, but Hattie did not notice. She stood still and said, "I want to see that bird, and I'm scared to, too."

"Oh, go on," Ruth Edna said roughly.

Hattie rounded the corner of the house and cried, "There he goes!" She went in pursuit and presently came from beneath the house, bony rear first, a chicken feather caught in her hair, presenting the bird dustily. "Look a-here. Sick eye."

Ruth Edna stepped back a nose length. "He don't look no different to me."

"No diff-e-runt! Don't you remember how his feathers used to shine in the sun, all colors of the rainbow!"

"Well," Ruth Edna said, thinking he did sort of look like the stuffed owl she'd had in the attic twenty-five years.

Hattie put the rooster down, and he ran on buckling legs, falling from one side to another, as if there were something in his stomach heavy as a bowling ball. "He's not long for this world," Ruth Edna said. "Let's face it."

"But, Ruth *Ed*—na!" Hattie said.

"Well, I got to go. I got a sick human to look after, you know. Give him a little whisky in a eye dropper."

"Why, I don't have any whisky," Hattie said.

86

"Hattie——" Ruth Edna said.

"Well, how much?"

"Oh, let him live while he can!" Ruth Edna went out to the yard and waved back gaily.

Hattie stood on the steps and watched her go, an emptiness in her heart. In all fairness, she told herself, Ruth Edna was exactly what Cotter said she was: the meanest woman alive, white or colored.

Fall was hinted at in the chrysanthemums, budding lavender in Brother Patrick's yard, in the browning zinnias, in the last of the flaming orange marigolds, their shaggy heads drooping. During the long, overgrown summer the citrus smell of mock orange had filled the air; now that languid smell was lost on an air crisp and sharp with the aroma of leaves beginning to dry. The sky, a blue as pure as the blue of the morning glory, had about it a sheen as white as in the throat of the flower. The sun bounded off the splintery gray-white walk, so blinding that Ruth Edna stepped down from it and walked in the middle of the road. Like Jake, she thought, and half expected to meet him coming the other way. But it was noon. There was no one in the road and no one in any of the five stores. Miss Alma, having left the post office, was in her house next door. At the gas station, Homer Brown's sign hung out: BLOW YOUR HORN LOUD. It meant he was next door having his dinner. Even the dust was settled. It hung on the trees, overshadowing the road in scoops as neat as if they had been placed there by hand. Chickens had settled into the shade under houses. In her whole vista the only sign of life was a brown-and-white hound curled onto itself in sleep in the middle of the road. Passing the post office, she glanced into the little room and saw in the one chair the old man past ninety who came in from the country to spit in the brass spittoon. He had just done so and turned and met her gaze, his eyes the same lusterless brown color as the tobacco, the juice hanging in drops on his yellowed beard. "How you, old man?" Ruth Edna said, stepping to the porch.

No part of him altered. She said, "You reckon we ever going to get a rain?"

The old man drew his arm quietly, as a bow, across his mouth, lowered his chin, and fell asleep. Sighing, Ruth Edna turned and watched a car approach. It was Wilroy and Mary Margaret, on their way to Memphis. They twiddled their fingers in goodbye as they passed. She tried to think how long it had been since she had gone anywhere in that car and figured it was six months ago to the revival of *Rebecca* in Senatobia; but then Mary Margaret had carried the whole Wednesday Eve Bible Class too.

Their dust flying behind settled into an eddy about her feet, stilled itself finally, and lay thick and soft as flour over them. Then she started home.

In the distance dustless trees were still as the town, still as the road and the yards and the houses with their occupants napping on full stomachs. The sky was blue and the trees turning all colors; browns were in the road and in the spots of the dog that lifted its head now and looked at her. Her world, so still, seemed one of dream.

Far away down the road, thinly on the still air, came the sounds of children at noon recess at the schoolhouse. Almost without thinking, she went toward the sound, her arms falling weightlessly in time to her walk, past the Methodist church, square as a child's building block, past the only concrete steps in town, leading up to Miss Loma's house.

When she arrived at the schoolhouse, perspiration stood on her forehead like rain. The play yard stretched ahead, vast as a desert to cross and just as grassless. Feeling shy, she crossed it, grateful to the children who spoke to her. She reached the building and pulled open the heavy door, escaped into the dark stuffy interior and followed the locker-lined corridor to steps in the distance, descended them as the cool concrete smell of the basement and the smell of spaghetti sauce rose to meet her.

In far corners of the cafeteria two girls, their hair straggling out of nets, wiped tables to a sticky cleanness. Ruth Edna crossed the room to the steam table and looked down into deep aluminum wells dried with spaghetti sauce; then she looked up at the two women who stood behind them with dripping faces. "Whew, you-all sure picked a hot day for spaghetti," she said.

"Afternoon, Miss Ruth Edna," said one woman.

"We run out of thinking up things to eat," said the other. "No two kids like the same thing anyway."

"Is that a fact?" Ruth Edna said. She looked into the kitchen. "How you, Waddie Mae?"

Waddie Mae, washing dishes, said, "All right, Miss Ruth Edna. How you?"

"Doing all right, I reckon. Hot."

"Huh, you don't know nothing," said one woman. She unbuttoned her uniform, exposing a wet pink slip, and disappeared into the closet to change; she could hear from there.

"I was just passing. I wondered if you-all might be shorthanded. I could help out," Ruth Edna said.

"Why, you're mighty sweet, Miss Ruth Edna," said the remaining woman. "But we ain't got any funds to hire more help."

"I don't need no salary really."

In the kitchen, Waddie Mae took her hands out of the water and listened.

"I'm sorry——" the woman said.

"It don't make any difference," Ruth Edna said. Her fingers clutched at the pink roses bordering her dress. Now she heard the silence in the closet, in the kitchen, in the far corners of the room. When she turned, the girls bent to their wiping again. "I better get on."

"Come eat lunch with us some day," the woman said. "We got so many potatoes from the government they're rottin' back there. The government ain't got sense God give a flea. Waddie Mae, you take you home a sackful today, hear?"

"Oh, I might do it sometime," Ruth Edna said.

She threaded her way out among the empty tables in total silence. Before the door fell to, she heard the woman come out of the closet and say, "It's a shame she's so———"

"Shhh," the other woman said.

Heads bent to their desks, children raised cautious eyes toward her from beyond the glass of the doors. She kept her eyes straight ahead until she reached the yard again, a relief after the stale interior. On the empty, quiet playground only a patent-leather belt lay, lost. About her the whole countryside was quiet.

Let 'em laugh, she thought, stepping up onto the walk. She had decided on a short way home, not wanting to be again the only person in town at noon. Her way led across pasture land and along a barbed-wire fence. In the whole of the way she would walk there was but one tree, an enormous maple just beginning to yellow for autumn. Beyond, ranged along a high bank, was the back of town, like a miniature of itself. She saw Miss Alma, a tiny figure, come to her back door and throw out a basin of water. Ruth Edna made her way toward the tree and stood on the side of it away from town, withdrew from the bosom of her dress a bottle containing the last of two ounces of paregoric, all you could get from the drugstore in Senatobia without a prescription.

There was a Negro man who got it for her as often as he could without arousing suspicion. His name was Little T., and she paid him a quarter for doing it. He was trying to save up enough money to buy a fishing lure, but it seemed to Ruth Edna he never got ahead. She was sorry for him, but it suited her purposes fine. She drank the medicine and stood shuddering until the moment of its taste was over, telling herself again, It's all Poppa's fault.

At forty-nine, he had had a stroke and for ten years had been her care, no more than a baby. Momma, from the first, had surrendered herself to despair. Memory as well as paregoric made Ruth Edna nauseous now; his diapers particularly had repelled her. Cotter, working in the fields in those days, had rested when he came home, but her work never ended.

Poppa had ruined other men for her, he had been so disgusting. (She was ashamed of the word, but was there another?) He cried out when she changed his diapers as if the whole sorrow of his sickness lay there. Once he even reached toward her in such a way she drew back instinctively, horrified. Afterward she told herself it couldn't have been; you never knew for sure what he wanted; he had lost the power of speech too. Despite his sickness, the end came unexpectedly. About to serve him breakfast one morning, she saw him slip away in an instant, just like that. It had haunted her for years that all she thought in the moment afterward was, If this isn't just like something that would happen to me. She had spent the previous day in its entirety peeling, coring, cooking enough apples to make him sauce for six weeks. Too innocuous for anyone else, it had remained on the shelf to spoil in its own time.

But nothing had ended with Poppa's death; Momma started in immediately. She stopped eating, saying first it was because her teeth didn't fit; next it was because her bowels couldn't pass anything. All that had been really wrong was, she was nutty as a fruitcake.

As soon as she got Momma to the grave, Cotter started. He said something was wrong with his chest. All her life had been waiting on other people. She'd never done anything in the world she wanted to do.

She had not cried when either of them died. But now in this lonesome lowering afternoon, thinking of ghosts, she was overcome with regret at her bitterness during those lost years. She cried aloud, longingly, after thirty-four years of silence, Poppa! Momma! and she forgave them at that instant not only their illnesses but their deaths as well.

Now she was drowsy and should be home. She started, and uptown Homer Brown's fice spotted her and came tremulously to the edge of the bank, barking shrilly. She hurried away in the opposite direction, following a faint path through recently crushed grass without knowing where the path was going. She was surprised, rounding a gully, to come upon Jake's house.

Black against the sun's angle, it stood, weather-beaten, like a discarded bird's house: small, oblong, unpainted. Against the golden afternoon the windows reflected round and black as holes; they seemed to know only what was inside them, like the eyes of the old.

Through one she glimpsed Jake a moment before she went on, her heart caught in her throat. Of all the people in the world, perhaps only Jake was worse off than she. Maybe doing for him was a second chance, to make up for all the meanness she had shown the others: Poppa, Momma, Cotter, even Hattie.

She stopped once more to take out the paregoric, run her tongue around the top of the bottle, and replace the cap. Then she went on, fearing now that she would be seen as she scaled the high bank into town, clinging to clumps of grass and to young trees. But she arrived on the main road, breathless and unnoticed, and passed along it to the road that led off to her house. When she arrived, Cotter was sitting on the porch, as he had been since noon, expecting his midday dinner.

He was starving, he said. *Star*—ving.

He expected Ruth Edna to say, Well, he wasn't helpless in the kitchen. To his surprise, she said she had some good tomatoes, spring onions, and cold corn bread; she'd fix something. When he came

94

along to the kitchen later, she had everything on the table, plus some warmed-up crowder peas. When they had almost finished eating, he said, "That idiot came by while you were gone."

"What idiot?"

"How many idiots you know around here?"

"Several."

"Now, Ruth Edna."

"If you mean Jake, how do you know he's a idiot? How do you know what Jake knows?"

"It ain't what he knows. It's what he don't know."

"What'd he want?"

"Who, the idiot? How do I know what he wanted. He just looked all around—for you, I guess—and left."

"Poor thing."

"Poor thing!" Cotter looked significantly at his nearly buttonless shirt. "I'd like to be poor thing a while."

"Well, be poor thing a while," Ruth Edna said, yawning, "but I'm going to take a nap." She got up and crossed the room to her bed and lay down.

Cotter had noticed for some minutes that she was about to fall asleep. He got up from the table and went slowly to the door, let it slam shut and went down the breezeway asking himself again, What in the dickens is wrong with Ruth Edna? She was all the time getting so groggy it was as if she wasn't even in the world. He'd thought for a time maybe she had hold of some whisky. But as Wilroy pointed out, Where would she get it? Maybe it was one of those confounded laxatives she was all the time taking.

He suddenly stepped up his shuffle and went off hurriedly, having just remembered it was the night they played pitch up to Miss Loma's store.

When Ruth Edna woke, it was to someone calling her name, ever so softly and fearfully. For a moment, she could not come to her senses and lay in the near-dark looking about. At the window the oak died brilliantly in the last light, its turned foliage casting a red glow into the room that lay on the far wall like firelight.

"Miss Ruth Edna." The voice came again softly.

She swung her feet quickly, heavily to the floor and stood up. "Little T.?" she said aloud.

"Yes 'um." The voice was still hesitant.

"There's nobody else here," she said, in a full voice. She crossed the room to the window and looked down at him. She could just make out his face in the end of evening light. And it was wet with sweat because he was afraid. The evening itself was cool.

She saw him relax a little.

"You going to Senatobia?" she said.

"Yes 'um. Mr. Wilroy, he say I can catch a ride with him sometime. I told him I had to go up there to see my Aun-tie. She's sick."

Ruth Edna turned back to the room and crossed it, searched for her pocketbook, and when she found it, took out a dollar and fourteen cents. She creased the dollar around the change until it all was the size of a penny. Then she carried him the money. She unlatched the screen and pushed it open with her hand wide enough to hand him the money. Ever since waking, she had had a disturbed, reluctant feeling, as if she had to see someone she did not want to. But when Little T. reached out and took the money, his hand touched hers slightly, and she felt no desire to recoil. It was not him, then, she did not want to see.

"When you bring it," she said, "Thursdays are a good night. Mr. Cotter is uptown to the card game."

"Yes 'um. Evening, Miss Ruth Edna." He touched a cap he wore.

"Goodbye, Little T.," she said.

As soon as he stepped back, he disappeared into the dusk. She heard him stumble once, right himself, swear softly and go on. She could not help but smile as she closed the window and returned to the room.

She lit one lamp and took Jake's shirts from the cedar chest and began to mend them. There was a smoky smell to them still from all the wood fires over which his momma had washed them in her black iron pot. Her perfect even stitches had long ago turned the collars and made patches that were almost invisible. Ruth Edna stared at the dead woman's handiwork, thinking of all that lost love and devotion. She wanted to cry, not knowing whether it was for Jake or his momma or herself. She felt devoid of bitterness, felt only a tired emptiness, and knew that the person she had not wanted to see upon arising had been herself.

Among the shirts some were beyond repair, and she wondered if she couldn't make Jake a shirt. She put down the finished mending and went outside. Flimsy as gauze, a little blue was left high up in the sky. It would gray soon and turn to dark too. In the garden a brown rabbit sat on its haunches, chewing tender greens, and stared at her. Who would fix the fence? she wondered.

She went out to the garden, and the rabbit ceased to chew, shuddered and bounded away. She lifted the crumpling gate and went in. Cotter, she noticed, had begun to tie up the tomato plants and had abandoned them to cascade, heavily laden, to the ground. Over the ragged row of greens she stood and looked at where the rabbit had chewed. She bent and began to pick, her fingers seeking expertly the youngest, tenderest leaves. She was going to cook Cotter a good supper tonight; she would cook the greens with a whole chunk of salt pork, the way he liked, instead of just with bacon grease. She'd even open some preserved thing that had been given them, instead of saving everything for holidays the way she had always done. Not until her lap was full of the dark gritty leaves did she look up.

Now dark had come. Only vague night-white clouds remained in the sky. She felt almost afraid beneath the giant canopy of night. She had a sudden desire to pray, but didn't know what to pray for. Finally she said, "Help all the sick folks."

In the trees a few shrill locusts screamed. In the lettuce crickets cried, and faintly off in the orchard. Nothing was visible but the white of her own hands, and she seemed to be following them as she went back to the house. She lit a lamp in the kitchen and, glad of the quick yellow flame, she lit one in Cotter's room and in the front room too. She washed the greens and put them on to cook. They would take a long time, and supper would be quite late. She heard footsteps along the breezeway and, carrying the lamp, went toward the dining room. "Cotter, is that you?"

There was no answer.

Fearful, she called again, "Cotter!"

She came all the way into the dining room before she saw Jake. He stood outside the screen door, his nose pressed against it. His eyes followed the lamp.

"Oh, Jake. Come on in." She motioned for him to open the door.

He came in, closed the door carefully behind him and stood just inside.

She gathered up the shirts. "You came too soon.

I was going to wash these for you. How often does that girl do them? It don't seem like these have been done lately."

She knew he did not understand a word, but she was glad of the sound of her voice in the room; it made this time seem more sociable.

"You know what I'm going to do?" she said, crossing the room. She held a shirt up against him, trying to get some idea of his measurements. Suddenly, without thought or intent, she stood on tiptoe and kissed him lightly. She held him about the neck an instant, quite strongly.

In that instant, she smelled the far-away smell of the hen house, but also something sweet. Stepping back, she saw jelly in the corners of his mouth.

While she watched, there appeared instead the drivel of his thick, foamy saliva.

She thought he was startled. "Jake——" she said.

Then she saw it was more than that. He had the look of an animal chased and caught.

He was terrified.

She put out her hands, but he was gone.

She followed him and was all the way to the front steps before she saw him. He had cleared the yard and jumped the fence. The shirt, caught on him somehow, floated behind in the night like a ghostly thing.

"Jake," she called. "I didn't mean . . ."

Her voice fell away sorrowfully on the night

air. She found it again and called again. "It was only me. Only Ruth Edna. . . ."

Her arms went out to the night and returned to her as they always had, empty.

5

Billy Morgan pushed his chair back from the supper table and said angrily to his wife, "All right. All right." He pushed an arm into each sleeve of a light sweater and scowled as he zipped it. "I'll be playing pitch at your momma's store," he said, and was careful to slam the front door leaving the house.

Frances forgot instantly what they had argued about. Now that he was gone, she was in a hurry. She cleared the table quickly and said to her three-year-old son, "Eat!" in a shout reduced to a sound like steam escaping.

Billy Jr. tried and failed, dropped his spoon into the little well of gravy he had made in his mashed potatoes.

"Oh, God!" Frances said.

She went to the kitchen and returned with a sponge, wiped at the gravy spatters hurriedly while they became circles of grease widening one upon another, giving a dull glaze to the shiny blond furniture. Not that she cared.

Billy had picked out the furniture, and it was his as far as she was concerned. They had argued over it bitterly as they had argued over everything. All they had ever agreed on was getting married. Why that had been was the kind of thing one could go on asking oneself afterward forever, when it was too late.

Carrying the wet sponge, she went to the window, glanced out and saw Cotter May hurrying up the road to her mother's store: Miss Loma's, where the pitch game was held every Thursday night. She stared at what she could see of the store's lights, as if she might will Frank to leave. But it was too early. He could never leave before seven thirty; now it was six. Waiting out the week between the Thursday nights when he slipped away from the game to come to her was almost more than she could bear.

At forty-four, Frank Patrick was fourteen years older than she. She remembered him first as a gangly boy coming to Sunday dinner with his parents, Brother and Mrs. Patrick. By the time she was grown, Frank was married. But in Marigold's limited social circles, he was considered still a "young married" when she entered that group. It was the group's custom to follow about on Saturday nights the dances that moved around the countryside from one lodge hall to another: Sarah, Sardis, Savage, Senatobia, Hernando and Marigold it went.

On these evenings she found herself increasingly in Frank's company. At first it was not so much by design as by circumstance. They liked the same tunes for dancing and preferred sitting for long periods of the evening merely watching, sometimes not even speaking. Most of the women did not drink at all, but Frances enjoyed moderate drinking very much, and it was companionable as they sat at the table together. To her, they had kindred senses of humor. She said to him once, "I think we're soulmates."

He looked perplexed, said nothing, but put out an arm and gave her a surreptitious hug.

After a particularly bitter fight with Billy one Saturday, she cried out, "Oh, if only we could get free of each other!"

And he said, "Well, we never will. We're going to stick this out for the kids."

Frances fell onto the bed, a heap of despair, and asked herself, Am I going to live forever, then, without love?

That evening, dancing with Frank, she suddenly moved closer and lifting her face, put it against his. He tightened his arm about her, more quickly than she could have hoped had she planned beforehand what she was going to do. They ceased to dance except in a parody of it, a reason for standing pressed together as they were in the middle of the floor.

She whispered, "I never thought that you . . ."

"Oh Jesus——." He let out his breath as if he had

been holding it a long while.

They left the floor and went out onto the porch where only lights treated against bugs burned, giving off a murky orange glow. I'll look terrible, she thought, like I don't have any lipstick on.

They stood close and stared at one another, prolonging the moment before they would kiss for the first time. When they had kissed, she thought, He's wonderful! They kissed again, and she put out her tongue and gave him a little lick about the chin and said, "Oh Frank, you're so sweet."

Entwined, they went out into the night, and as though through a maze, went about the parking lot seeking his car. Then he stood with his hand on the door handle and said, "I don't want to do it in a car. I haven't done that since I was sixteen. But there's no place else, and I don't want to wait."

"Oh, no. Don't wait."

What if he doesn't like me, she thought. What if I'm like I am with Billy. Suddenly she was afraid. What if I am cold?

But she was not.

She cuddled up to him and said, "Frank, was I all right?"

"All right? Baby, you were swell."

"Swell——. My husband thinks I'm cold."

"Cold! What the hell does he expect? You're hot as a little firecracker."

"I *am* cold with him. He just never has been able to make me feel the way I did with you just now."

"Well Jesus, I'm sorry."

"So am I," she said, and tried to smile.

Presently, he said, "I could do it all over again. How 'bout you?"

"I could. But we don't have time." She sat up and bit at his ear. "In fact, we've been gone so long now, I'm scared. We'd better hurry."

They got out of the car and went back hurriedly the way they had come. She kept thinking, Now I'm really me. She felt she had been a girl when she came to the dance, but that she would go home a woman. And not a cold one either, she told herself happily.

"Have you done anything like this before?" she said.

He gave her a little slap on the behind and winked. He lit a cigarette, and in the match's flare she saw gray where his hair was beginning to turn at the temples. She thought this was thrilling. Beneath his eyes was a slight puffiness that had come with age, and she thought this was thrilling too. Oh, I'm going to love him so, she thought. He's so cute.

"Frank, what are we going to do?"

"I don't know. I'll have to figure out something. I'd sure like to see you again."

"I have to see you. You just don't know."

They had come to the lodge. Faintly above the door in the dark the white V.F.W. letters stood out. He said, "You'd better go around to the side entrance, like you've been to the women's toilet. I'll stay here and smoke like I've been here all the time."

They separated, and when they met again inside, she sat with her eyes on him the rest of the evening.

They did not meet again for many weeks, not until Billy and several others went duck hunting. Then Frances went into the yard early and stayed close by the fence setting out tulip bulbs. As she had known he would, Frank passed by close to ten o'clock on his way to get the mail. When she waved, he pulled his pick-up truck to the side of the road immediately.

"Good morning," she said. "I thought maybe Eleanora was with you. I wanted to ask her something about these bulbs. She always has such a pretty garden."

"No, she's home."

"I'm surprised you didn't go to Stuttgart with the rest of the gang."

"I don't care too much for duck hunting."

"Oh, is that right? Well, it's a nice little overnight trip anyway."

"That's so," he said. He tipped his hat. "I'll tell Eleanora you want to ask her something about the garden. Nice to see you, Frances." He drove away.

Did I make a fool out of myself? she wondered. Did he understand? Does he care?

But it was no more than an hour before he arrived in her kitchen, freshly washed and shaved, having come up the back way. With few words, they went to bed. Briefly she wondered if that was all she meant to him. Am I just a slut? she asked herself. Why don't I care that it's in Billy's own bed?

But thinking their love was beautiful, she did not care. Her anguish at last was put to rest. Later he made his way out again successfully the way he had come. They had hit upon Thursday nights as their only solution: Billy would be out of his house, Frank would have an excuse for leaving his. There would be risks. Suppose her mother or a neighbor dropped by? Suppose Eleanora found out he left the game early each week? They felt them risks worth taking.

She looked at herself now in a new light. Before, she had been always ready to criticize others. Now she was what they called "the other woman." She had done what they called "stealing love"— but she had needed the love so much. If she had stolen food for her starving children, would anyone have thought it wrong? Wasn't it almost the same?

Darkness had come into the room and dusk to the world outside. Street lights made lonesome islands of light. How peculiar that the two men were there playing cards together: the one, a stranger to whom she had been married for five years; the other, who had only had to kiss her once for her to belong to him entirely. She felt she had belonged to Frank forever, even while she was still in the region

108

of darkness and he was born.

When she turned back to the room, Billy Jr. sat still with his supper unfinished. She took away his plate to the kitchen and washed the dishes quickly, furtively, as if Billy might suddenly look over her shoulder. He made the child eat everything on his plate, always! If he were allowed to goof off now, he might goof off forever, he said. Billy had so many rules, Frances' head ached sometimes trying to keep up with them all.

Her momma had warned her against marrying a Yankee, even though Billy was a child when his poppa, a widower, had moved to Marigold from upper New York State where he had failed at growing apples. Billy had told her what he remembered of the winters there, how the snows had piled on top of one another and stood in dirty heaps, till April sometimes.

April! She had said it in astonishment, thinking what the word meant to her: japonica red as a sunset, fragile dogwood and grass as green and shiny as the shredded kind you put into children's Easter baskets. And the air! as soft as the tread of a kitten's paws, as sweet as their little faces.

Billy said they had trudged to school through tunnels dug in the snow, the snow flung on either side making banks taller than the children's heads.

Why, she had said, didn't they just stay home the way children in Marigold would have done? Shoot, Yankees just liked to make things hard for themselves. Who in Marigold would have dug through all that snow? Nobody she could think of. It would have been a time for sitting before the fire, popping corn and playing Rook.

She thought it was this feeling of basic alienness from Billy that accounted for the intensity with which she had fallen in love with Frank. She felt she had come home again, back to her own people, back to their ways. Sometimes, lying awake at night, she would think, All that snow, all that cold; it was bound to make a person harder, gruffer, different. She would sleep, to dream that the snow lay next to her in a frozen mound, untouchable.

"Bed," she said to Billy Jr. He put up his little arms, and she carried him into the bathroom and then to bed. He had to be asleep before Frank came. "Hurry now, hurry," she said anxiously, while he selected from among a jungle of toys something to sleep with. Then he was beside the bed, and she knelt with him while he said, in his baby's voice, "Now I lay me down to sleep. . . ."

She took him into her arms afterward. He was so slight, so tiny, she thought how easily his little bones could break beneath the pressure of her arms. "Oh, my teeny bones, my little boy," she said, and was overcome with sorrow at the void in her life. If only the man she loved were the father of her children . . .

When he was in bed she stood a moment and looked at Judy in her crib, her limbs flung wide in sleep, the bottle she had sucked dry resting on one shoulder. Frances moved it slightly, not far. If Judy woke in the night, she had to find it.

She returned to the living room, forlorn with her own unhappiness, aware more than ever of the dimension Frank added to her life. She stared about the room, depressed by it. Once decorating the house had been a consuming interest, but her interest had diminished at the exact pace of her interest in the marriage. Where she had taken the last brushstroke of a new coat of paint halfway up the molding in the hall was evident. She regarded it now as a sort of measure, the way people kept records of children's heights on the walls. Perhaps the day she left off painting was the day she had decided she was never going to like going to bed with Billy. Perhaps it was the day he had said never again ask him how much money he made or he would never give her any.

At the window, she held aside the lifeless marquisette curtain and, looking out, saw only the empty road. She returned to the center of the room, listening for sounds from the children's room. Only a moment before she had heard great zoomings and *ka-tows*, a great many soldiers were meeting their deaths, but now it was quiet. Her heart beat fearfully. She went about the house turning off lights, except for one in her bedroom. She stood in the darkened hallway, waiting, thinking, Suppose it's tonight we are caught?

Then he opened the door. In two strides, she was down the hall. She threw her arms about him and said, "Honey. Oh, honey."

They went into the bedroom and sat opposite each other while she told him all she had done during the week. The long week. He told her of the evening, that he had held bad cards and had been glad to leave. Oh, she teased, was that the only reason?

He never mentioned Billy, and she seldom spoke of Eleanora. It was the only area of shyness left between them.

He removed his shirt and his shoes, and she thought how once she had been embarrassed even by that. She had wanted them only in bed and making love, with no preliminaries—nothing to be unbuttoned, unzipped, removed, no words. She had been unrealistic, childish. Now the fact that these ordinary things had to happen between them gave her pleasure. It made their love-making even more extraordinary.

When Frank removed his undershirt, she came to him, knelt and put her head against his chest, touched the hair there. He put his hand on the side of her head and held her to him, making her feel quite small. She heard only a sound like that in a sea shell. She considered it her special world; she could smell his soap and his skin, and she thought, I have come home. Thank you, God.

"What?" She sat up and took down his hand.

"I said, 'I have to go to the bathroom.'" He grinned.

While he was gone, she removed everything but her slip and was in bed when he came back. She did not like to be seen naked until they were actually making love, but she was glad he had no embarrassment. He walked without clothes to the dresser and put down his change and his keys and his wallet. Just as Billy does every night, she thought; how often she had watched him.

Looking at Frank now, she could not help but compare him to Billy. Twelve years' difference in age made a difference. Though Frank was thin, he was slightly flabby, though in good condition. For someone his age, she thought automatically, surprising herself. It was the first time she had felt in the least separate from him, or realized that they did, after all, belong to different generations.

He came to bed with a cigarette and crushed it out in an ashtray on the bedside table. "Remind me to empty that," she said. "Billy's started in on those filter tips."

Surely, he made love to her. She responded so passionately she would have been embarrassed had he ever shown the least inclination to be so. But she had promised herself not to hold back here, not the only place in the world she felt she had ever been herself. Only in childbirth had she ever been taken out of herself before. And then, catapulted into pain, she had cried out helplessly, against her will.

It had outraged her to submit to pain. But not to love.

"It was wonderful," she said. "Was it for you?"

"Sure," he said. "You're sure something."

"Do you think my fanny's too big? Billy does."

"I think it's fine." He patted it.

"What are you thinking about?"

"Nothing. I'm just tired."

But she thought it was more than that. "Is it about us? Are you worried about us?"

"No," he said. "Everything's just the same between us."

"Hopeless?" she said, and was sorry. She had promised not to talk any more for a while about their getting divorces. He had said she could not understand what it was to have been married for twenty years, how much you had tied up in it— there were children and a house and property and a great span of shared experiences.

But she had not wanted to think practically and had been somewhat disappointed that he did. She wanted to run through town and cry, Yes, we're cheating. And I love it!

Didn't he realize how exceptional their love was? She had once read an expression she thought somewhat trite: A happy marriage can never be broken up. Suppose it were true?

"I'm sorry," she said. "I said I wouldn't talk about us any more for a while."

114

He touched her. "I was thinking about chickens."

"Chickens!" My God, she thought, he had been thinking about chickens while she was trying to solve their whole lives. That was the advantage men had over women—their work. They could always worry about it instead of something they couldn't do anything about.

"I'm going to have to start raising them, now that cotton's limited. Folks seem to be doing right well with them, but I hate the dirty bastards."

"I too," she said. "We were thinking of rice. But it seems like so much work."

"Don't it, though. I wish I could give up farming altogether and raise only cattle. That's all I really ever have cared about, cattle."

She was sitting up, leaning against her knees. She wondered if he were looking at her, and at that moment he ran his hand the length of her back. "You're nice," he said.

She wanted desperately to turn to him again, but as always, there was not enough time. "I guess we'd better get up," she said.

"I reckon so." He slid from the bed and went again into the hall to the bathroom.

She dressed while he was gone. When he returned, she sat on the bed and watched him. It's so long till next Thursday, she thought, and pressed her hand against her mouth, thinking she was going to cry out. He could not possibly know how much these evenings meant to her. She had discussed with him briefly her problems with Billy but never had told him how unsatisfactory everything really was. If Frank knew how completely she was his, he would begin to lose interest. It was only human nature.

She wondered if he would possibly go home and make love to Eleanora tonight. She wondered how often he did, anyway. She had always wanted to ask him but would not. Several times she had awakened in the night abruptly with a feeling of total loss. Each time she had traced the feeling back to a dream of Frank making love to Eleanora. At those times she had looked at Billy sleeping beside her and been glad that he was there.

Faintly, far off, the church bell began to ring nine o'clock. "We'd better hurry," she said. "I'll walk a little way with you."

"Good," he said.

She stood on tiptoe and kissed him about the mouth and chin as he put on his coat. They went arm in arm out into the night. One cloud covered the moon and shone luminously, blue; the sky looked thick and dark as midnight. Frances wondered if it were going to rain tomorrow. They followed the uneven wooden walk, crossed the road, and gained the walk on the other side. Ahead were two houses dark as shut-up boxes. They passed them and moved freely down the un- inhabited road. Only the Mays' was beyond. At a bend they stood to separate. He would cut across a field here that would take him home without having to pass back through town. He put his head down to kiss her and raised it suddenly. "What was that?"

"What was what?"

"Somebody yelling," he said.

She heard it too. They completed the bend and were facing the Mays'. Against the lighted front windows, they saw a man running across the yard. He cleared the fence as Ruth Edna came onto the porch.

"What——?" Frank said. He started forward. Frances caught him back. "She's all right," she said. "She's calling him back. Who is it? Could it be Cotter?"

"Why would he be running? Maybe it's somebody going to get Cotter."

At that moment the feet came toward them on the gravel quicker than it seemed possible for them to have covered that distance. They drew back from the road instinctively. At the last moment Frank stepped forward, but he glimpsed only something white. Then they were listening again to the sound of feet running on gravel, already some distance away.

"What in God's name? Did you hear it?" Frank said.

"I heard something, but it couldn't have been a man."

"It must have been. But it sounded like something half crazy looking for water."

"What are we going to do?"

"It—he headed uptown. We better go see, unless we ought to go see about Miss Ruth Edna."

"She seems all right. She went back in the house. How could we explain it if we went to ask her?"

"Let's go," he said. They began to run, sometimes together, sometimes with Frances lagging behind. He reached the corner just before her, and when she came up, they stared uptown as the door of her mother's store opened; the men came tumbling out. All along the way cautious doors were being opened and lights were coming on. Frank said, "You better go home. I'll go see." Without another word he went off.

She knew as precisely what to do as if someone had handed her instructions. She did not particularly like herself for knowing. Hurrying home, she wondered which person was herself: this one who knew what to do now, who cared about nothing but herself and Frank, or the guiltless half-person she had been before.

Entering the house, she emptied the ash tray Frank had used, straightened the bed and flung an opened magazine on it. She turned on lights in the hall, in the living room, on the front porch, and looked in on the children before she left the house again.

"What is it?" she called, recognizing Ed Veazey ahead of her on the walk.

"Don't know," he called back, and went on almost faster than he could, his chin drawn in, his chest thrust out, comical as someone in a walking race.

The night was alive now with people. All along the way, doors stood open, porches, living rooms, yards were lighted. Frances had never in her life been afraid of the dark night roads, but she was afraid of them brightly lit. It was as if the world had blown up, and everyone were running to survive. There seemed no time to stop, and as she ran, she was aware of the street lights standing out from everything, spots of white-hot color above the road, naked and alone. A nucleus of people had formed in the road ahead, and she ran toward it as if her safety lay there, though actually that was where the unknown, possibly the danger, lay. Around in her mind went the phrase, crazily, Safety in numbers, safety in numbers.

Oh, God, don't let it be Momma, don't let it be Billy, don't let it have anything to do with me at all, she thought.

Beyond, the countryside lay as it should, dark and serene. She thought of the people sleeping undisturbed. She thought of the grave on the nearby slope, with her father in it unaware, the flowers in the cylindrical cold metal vase sunk into the ground over his chest, making bright spots in the dark. On this strange night, she thought, even stranger things could happen; she stopped running, gazed eons away to the very faintly star-pocked sky, and whispered, "Daddy! Daddy, what is it like?"

Then she ran again toward the circle of people that was continually widening as the people stepped backward. It was as if they were going to catch hands and begin the steps of some old country folk dance they had rehearsed.

Beyond their heads she saw her mother and Billy with relief. She felt the crowd's fear now and heard again the sounds she and Frank had heard in the road. If it were a mad dog, why wasn't everyone running?

Jostling elbows, she pushed her way forward to the front of the circle and stood, seeing.

A feeling of revulsion went over her and the first faint stirrings of pity.

Behind her someone said, "I always did expect it."

She asked herself, Had she? She could only answer herself, No.

Jake, she had thought, would always be the same as she had known him. Perhaps that accounted for the feeling of mislaid trust she felt now as she watched him running about in the middle of the road, in circles of his own, foaming at the mouth. The sounds he made were his sounds of terror, but the crowd thought only of its own.

"Did you see him?" Lulu Veazey said to Frances. Before she could answer, Lulu said, "I never in my life! He came by my house faster than a jack rabbit.

And the noise! Worse, even, than he's making now."

Somebody else said, "My dog run out after him barking his head off. As soon as I saw good I run out and got him and tied him up. I told my husband at the time, Jake's as liable to bite that dog as the other way round."

"You mean like he was really mad?" said a thin trembly voice.

"Shoot," said the first.

"He was at my house this very afternoon," said Leila Brown, gaining everyone's attention. "The kids stopped him going by and commenced to joke with him, and I had him up on the porch and give him a Coke. He could have gone out of his head right there!"

"You might all be dead as doornails right now," somebody said.

"Ohh," everybody said.

"Think of all the times he's been around our kids," Leila said.

"Our girl children," said Kate French, with four hanging onto her arm, and big with a fifth child. "And clear out of his head all the time."

Her sister, Lucille Anderson, said, "You never know. It ain't safe, I tell you. The menfolks are going to have to do something."

"They will," said another woman. "Don't worry about that."

"Listen," somebody said.

The crowd had turned toward one man: old man

Hot Evans. It was the first time in two years he had been all the way to town. He stood wagging his billy goat's beard and said, "Mad. I seen 'um like this fifteen years ago when I took Sister Annie to the 'sylum. Crazy as bedbugs, some of 'em, just standing there banging their heads against stone walls till they bled, not even feeling it."

Everyone turned back and looked at Jake and could imagine him doing it.

Only Miss Loma and Mary Margaret Sheaffer stepped forward and did not want to believe it. Frances saw Wilroy grab them both back quick, like children not understanding danger and about to cross a street. Frances saw him say something to them in quick sharp words and they looked at each other and began to cry. They're wishing Jake's momma was here, Frances thought.

She saw Cotter May standing to one side with a whitened face, pressing his chest, still holding his card hand.

It had gone clear out of her head in the excitement. But of course it had been Jake that left Ruth Edna's! But if he had gone crazy at her house, why would she have just stood on the porch and called to him? Well, taking into consideration that sometimes Ruth Edna acted crazy herself, wouldn't she at least have gone to a telephone and called somebody? It was always her phone, the nearest one, that Ruth Edna used. It was strange, but it seemed almost as if Ruth Edna didn't want anyone to know he had been there.

The crowd had begun to thin slowly, and those who had come the farthest began to go home again, leaving what would happen to Jake to those who had always cared for him.

He had wound down like a top. He had sunk to the ground and fallen over on his side. He was not making the sounds any more, but was wet with long streaks of his own saliva, like a bloodhound or a horse. He half lay, half sat, panting. Slowly he began to look around, as if surprised to find himself back here after all that running.

Tentatively her mother and Mary Margaret and Wilroy began to approach him. She saw little old Miss Hattie McGaha hovering in the background, indicating she would be willing to help if only she had the courage. Some of the men went back to the card game. She saw Cotter give his hand to one of them. He said he was too worn out, and he had a ride home. He got into Freddie Moore's silver jalopy. She wanted to run after him and cry, "Find out from Ruth Edna!"

But how could she explain how she had known? Why would she have been out on that deserted road at night alone, the children left behind? She never had gone out walking by herself a time in her life. Suppose everybody else believed it? Billy wouldn't.

Across the cleared place around Jake she saw Frank. In the act of looking away from Jake he saw her.

She had to talk to him. Because it was implicit in the way that people were turning away and walking off, as if it were all decided, that something was going to happen to Jake.

She made her way around the circle and stood close to him and said, "That was Jake coming out of Ruth Edna's. Something must have happened to him there. We ought to tell somebody."

"I was thinking the same thing," he said. "Otherwise, why wouldn't she have come to town? She couldn't have helped but hear all these cars. And people have been shouting up and down the road. It's like a circus."

"I saw Darby Metcalf," Frances said. "If he heard, she's bound to have."

"Jesus," he said. "There's nothing we can say."

"Nothing?" she said.

They were separated by a little group tripping over one another as they got close to Hot, who was walking away telling something: something the old people seemed to know. It was evident in her mother's sorrowing face. Frances could tell she and Mary Margaret and Wilroy were discussing what to do with Jake tonight—before tomorrow? Tomorrow, she thought, afraid. It was going to sound funny if she and Frank waited until tomorrow to tell. He's the one ought to do it, she thought.

Men could get away with things like that better than a woman. There were a thousand things a man could say: that he was worried about money or crops and had gone off into the dark to think things out; that he had been feeling run-down and had drunk more beer than he had meant to and felt woozy and gone out for air. Or, if worse came to worst, just let people guess what he had been doing. People didn't think anything about a man; it was practically expected. The others would begin to put together all the Thursday nights and know it was not a sudden, urgent one-time thing, that he was carrying on an honest-to-goodness affair; but who would care besides Eleanora? And she could not leave him. No forty-year-old woman with the amount of money they had and four children was going to leave her husband for no more reason than that. And he could reason with her. He could say all the things that men said: that it had nothing to do with her; that a woman couldn't understand, it was just something that was in a man; that he was sorry and wouldn't do it again. She would forgive him. She might even forget. He could even say it was a Negro—one over in the cabins near the Metcalf's, and that would account for the way he had taken. Eleanora wouldn't care nearly so much if it was a Negro; she'd know it wasn't somebody he was in love with. She'd probably think she had failed him in some way, and she would try harder, and in the long run he'd benefit.

125

Men could never think up verbal deceits. She was going to have to tell him reasons. Wasn't Brother Patrick ever going away? "Good evening," she said. He had seen her staring at him.

"Good evening, Frances," he said. "Isn't this something?" He shook his head sadly. In the moment that he looked at Jake, Frances looked at Frank. He looked back at her with the same look of straining she had on her face. He's trying to give me a reason, she thought. She said, "There's nothing I can say."

He said, "Why not? Your mother's a friend of Ruth Edna and Jake too."

"But what difference does that make?" she said. "She doesn't know anything's wrong between me and Billy. I wouldn't even know where to begin trying to say something."

"I don't know anything to say either," he said. "And maybe all this would've happened no matter where he was."

"Maybe," she said, bitterly. "It's easier to think so."

He turned deliberately away. Furious, she went back around the circle and stared as if she could force him into action. He looked back at her with a look that said plainly, It's kind of disagreeable, isn't it, to think of that room back there and that messed-up bed?

Pale, wan as a moon against the dark night, his face stood out; she looked at it and thought all that she had taken for gentleness in him had been in reality wishy-washiness. He really was too short for her—or for anybody but that little squat wife of his.

Every time he looked at her he would think she was having an affair with someone else. She hated him for it already.

The night seemed so long it should be dawn. Instead it was only ten fifteen. There was a whole evening still to be got through. Billy was coming home now; she had seen him coming out of the store, putting on his sweater. There was nothing to do but meet him and go home with him. I've come back to you, Billy, she thought, even if you didn't know I'd ever been gone.

Tomorrow's breakfast coffee would be as bitter as the air between them, boiled because she would have been with the baby, who always made a mess in her pants at the wrong time. And she would not have a Thursday to look forward to, so that it wouldn't matter. Everything now would matter.

Eleanora had come up to Frank and put her arm through his. Now they were going home, and in passing Eleanora spoke. Frances spoke back, avoiding even looking at Frank. You should have done something, she said silently to his retreating back, her teeth ground together. Oh how lovey-dovey they were! How cute! He did love her, God damn it, even after twenty years. Oh, why doesn't someone love me? she thought. And why don't I love anybody? She had so much love to give.

Billy was helping her mother and Mary Margaret to lift Jake up; his legs kept buckling beneath him. Wilroy had gone to get the car. She approached them.

"Can you help us a minute?" her mother said.

She stood and began to cry convulsively, childishly and helplessly, letting her nose run. "I . . . can't . . ." she said finally.

"Oh, baby, it's all right," her mother said. She looked at Mary Margaret and said, "It's time for her to have the curse."

"Run on home, hon," Billy said, attempting sympathy. "The kids are liable to have waked up."

"Where are you taking him?" she said.

"To Whitehill to jail," her mother said. "Wilroy and Billy will have to drive him."

"What on earth are you taking him to jail for?" she said.

"Where else are we going to keep him?" Mary Margaret said. "We can't keep him our ownselves and risk being slit open in the night in our beds. Jake wouldn't go to, but then it would be too late to be sorry."

"And he can't stay by himself," her mother said. "He's liable to fall out again."

Wilroy came up then, and the women shifted their side of Jake onto him. The car door stood open waiting, the motor running fitfully like a panting dog.

She saw him last. He sat in the front by Wilroy who was driving. And Billy sat in the back to watch him. Patient: she had seen him squatting on his haunches beside a flower in bud as if waiting for it to bloom. Kind: he never had anything that he didn't offer it to others. And no one ever took anything from him. Children were taught never to take candy from Jake; he might have slobbered on it. Once she had come upon a colored girl sitting beside the road crying, half crazy because in passing Jake some of his slobber had accidentally got on her. It was the only time in her life Frances had ever wanted to say, Nigger. Nigger, get up out of the way and let me pass.

Her heart had been broken tonight; it was never going to heal.

Her mother had said something to her, and she and Mary Margaret had faded away into the darkness to close up the store.

She was alone in the road, in the night, in the world. The same as Jake, she thought, with everything she wanted to say locked up inside her.

6

Little T. saw two things that night. Going down the road from Ruth Edna's, he saw Jake standing some distance away, looking at the house as if trying to make up his mind about something. Little T. had been hurrying along as fast as possible, feeling the money in his hand, hard and firm, his hand already sweaty from gripping it. He did not see or hear anything until suddenly he was right on Jake. It almost scared the fire out of Little T.

"Uh!" he cried out, coming on the white face in the dark, feeling a body near.

When he saw it was Jake, he edged away and went on again at his fast quiet pace, knowing no one else would be on this road until Mr. Cotter came home from the card game. He did not think the loony man even saw him; he had only continued to look at the house and seemed to be telling himself something. Little T. had been afraid because it was the loony man. It was his first direct contact with

130

him. Yet he knew his safety lay in that fact: the man could not tell anything.

He saw the second thing when he reached the main road. He stopped before entering it and looked up and down, making sure the road was empty. Then he darted quickly across it to the safety of a dark store porch. Only the few street lights and the lights from Miss Loma's store, at the opposite end of town, illuminated the night. He was about to leave the dark safety and enter the shadows and gain another store porch, so making his way on out of town, when the door of Miss Loma's opened. A man came out walking slowly as if he were not going anywhere, gaining speed as he came. When he passed the store where Little T. stood, Little T. ceased to breathe, then resumed after he saw Mr. Frank Patrick pass by. Mr. Frank stopped before the Morgan house, looked around casually, hunched his shoulders and then went up the walk and into the house without knocking. Little T.'s eyebrows rose and fell. He was not surprised, because not too much surprised him, and he was interested only to the extent of confirming his suspicion; he stopped outside Miss Loma's window a moment and saw that Mr. Morgan was inside playing cards. Little T. had not been much interested in Jake, either. It was only later that he wondered about that.

All he was interested in was the spinning lure. He had seen it first two months ago, end of July, through the grayish glass of Miss Loma's showcase. Bright copper, it was splayed like an unloosed pin-wheel, so that at the first moment of his seeing it he had seen it also in his imagination twirling and shining through the opaque muddy waters of Arka-butla Creek. Rising slowly, it skirted the water's surface with a hop, skip, jump, so brightly flashing, so irresistible that Bessie, wherever she hid in that sluggish backwater, would be taken by surprise and wait and wait again for its reappearance, unable to resist the lure.

Ha!

He had reeled her in there in Miss Loma's on that hot July afternoon. She had tugged violently, head and tail alternating in breaking water, glim-mering darkly silver and then green against the astonishing blue of the summer sky. Mouth agape, neatly hooked through her bottom lip, she had walled toward him one terrified black, yellow-ringed eye. "No use, Cat," he said. "I got you now." He flopped her onto the bank where she lay apprehensively, her gills reddening, opening use-lessly. She had eluded him three years, and he fig-ured now, by this spring, she would be maybe ten pounds, worth waiting for.

He stepped close to Miss Loma's showcase and said almost in a whisper, "Miss Loma, how much that lure?"

"Boy, you can't afford that lure," Miss Loma said. She moved over to the case and slid it open, took out the cardboard and handed it to him. He put out a cautious finger and unhooked the lure. Beneath it he saw the price and whistled. "Seventy-five cents for one lure!" he said. It was not a question, but a concurrence: the lure was worth it. He knew right away he could catch the cat with it, and Miss Loma knew it too. "Little T., you're liable to catch that cat with that lure," she said.

Everybody knew of his persistence in trying to catch the cat. Others had tried, too, when she first appeared in these parts. There was something special about the way she chased bait and broke water with her head just as you reeled it in. Then she stared at you as if to say, I knew it. I was right not to take that.

She did this two or three times every season. Enough to let you know she was still there, enough to keep you fishing, and damned to catch her. In the early days she had been hooked two or three times and that was how she came to be known. But she always got off. No one ever landed her. No one doubted it was the same cat. There was to her whiskers a distinctive lilt and length, and she was unusually large, and eventually there were scars where the hooks caught her. But mostly her air of wisdom set her apart. Whoever sighted her first each year sang out loud along the bank for everybody to hear, "Heah Bessie back!"

Then little children hopped up and down, did dances like Indians and whooped and hollered. It

133

got so all they wanted to be when they were grown was the one who caught Bessie.

Catching her was the only thing Little T. had ever wanted to do in his life. Everything else he had ever done, he had done because he had had to: finish out the sixth grade, work and go into the Army. After he finished school, he worked at Mister Jordan Moody's where his mother was the cook. He had worn a little white jacket and helped to serve at the table. All the women guests would exclaim, "Now, if that's not *the* cu-test thing!" And he had felt like some kind of piss-ant.

Finally one of the men guests told him if they were him they'd go up to the Peabody Hotel in Memphis and get a job; they had boys no older than him waiting on tables, making good money. So he did, though his mother said all the time it was a mistake, and he was hired right away. He was told that if anyone asked him how old he was to say he was sixteen. He wondered who would believe it when he wasn't even formed as a man. Again, he found himself in a white jacket, but this time he was supposed to be going to make all this money. He made some, but it was all used up in living. Some of it went to a cousin as rent and there was carfare, clothes, picture shows, just things to do in Memphis. When he went into the Army, he had no more money than when he had started work. And he was back to doing things he didn't want to do. He certain to God did not want to go into the Army.

Right off, they asked him what his name was, what Little T. stood for. He had never wondered before. His daddy simply had been Big T. always, and he had been Little. He wrote his mother and asked, and she wrote back, Tom. In the Army they called him Tom. When he returned home again, he was called Little T. Either one, it made no difference to him, like a lot of things in life.

His mother had died and his daddy did nothing but fish. Little T., having no other ambitions, joined him. It was his daddy who first caught Bessie, and it was he who came the closest to ever landing her. It was he who named her. He caught her the first time bucking like a bronco on the end of the line, and he pulled her in gentle and easy saying, "Whoa there now, Bessie. Come ahead, girl." But she had slipped off sly as you please just as he drew her out of the water. It was as if she had been holding the hook in her mouth all the time, to let it go when she wanted. With a flip of her tail she flopped back into the water and was gone before either he or his daddy could say a word. Then they stood on the bank, slapping each other on the back, saying, "Man, oh, man!"

Now his daddy was dead. He found him one evening, a year ago this summer, with his pole in the water, his legs stretched out in front of him and his chin on his chest. He was leaning up against the side of the bank, the life just gone out of him. Little T. couldn't think of a better way in the world to go.

Little T. got fifteen dollars a month from the government and would for the rest of his life. It would have been enough for just him, but he had supported his daddy. Now he was so far in debt he knew he would never get out again. He was granted the money because of an accident in the Army. He was helping to load crates on a truck when suddenly the driver drove off, unexpectedly and with a jerk. Several of the crates toppled off onto Little T. It banged up his face, was all it did. But he lay in the hospital a month, tubes sticking out of his nose, down his throat, out of his head, anywhere they could stick any. He felt bad for a long time. Then he was well, and all he could think of was getting even with the driver, Duke Williams; he never would forget his name. He believed Duke had done it on purpose. They had, some time before, had a little argument over poker.

But Duke had been transferred while Little T. was in the hospital. He never saw him again. For a long time he would sometimes stop, a chill running through him, thinking he saw a familiar figure on the street. He would wait till the figure passed and peer close to make certain it was not Duke. It was one of the few times in his life Little T. had ever been possessed by a craze to do something; perhaps that was why the craze was so great. Now his desire for the lure was the same.

The Army doctors had done plastic surgery on his face. His nose was wider and flatter than it had been before and much less prominent. In winter he had trouble with his sinuses; his nose was still a little crooked and didn't drain just right. But he said, who cared? Shoot, for fifteen dollars a month and a rating of permanent disability, who minded losing a few teeth and not looking as pretty as some gal might like? He had a slight scar across his nose, and several people had asked if he were ever a boxer. That had pleased him. They would think probably that he had been a welterweight, possibly even a Golden Gloves champion.

After his daddy died, he lived on in the little place they had had. It was one room with a double bed, a couple of wicker chairs and a small wood stove. He cooked on the stove in the dead of winter, but he cooked outdoors when he could, on a little iron grill he had fashioned for his yard. Actually his yard was the whole bottomland, for he was the only person who lived in it. Others came only to fish and hunt. When he fished, Little T. carried with him a small black iron skillet, held to himself by a rope belt. He intended whenever he caught Bessie to sit right down and eat her. He even carried a small packet of seasoned corn meal to roll her in. And he had his own way of fashioning a little cookstove out of rocks and twigs. He would catch her. He was sure of it. And this coming spring, if he had that lure.

He was the only person fishing the bottomland who had a casting rod. Everyone else had a bamboo pole and used bait: shrimp, worms, bread, bugs, anything they could think of. Old Bald Dave was quite successful with potato chips.

Old Bald Dave was the only completely bald-headed Negro anybody in these parts had ever seen. He had lost his hair from a disease that had cleared up and left him with his shining head. Little T., joking, called him Eight Ball. Sometimes Bald Dave added more salt to the chips; other times he left them alone. Whatever, he always came up with a fish. He had told Little T., "You and your fancy pole. I'm going to catch that cat yet, with a old wore-out potato chip." But he never had, much to Little T.'s relief.

You could say one thing, though. Crappie sure went for potato chips. There was a big one on the line every time Bald Dave threw it in. He went all over town collecting left-over broken potato chips from picnics, church affairs, any kind of social. People saved them for him in greasy bags. It had made him a kind of character in the town, and once Little T. had heard two white men talking about it. "You ever seen that baldheaded nigger that comes around collecting old potato chips?" the first man asked.

"I hear he fishes with them," the second man said.

"Oh, you go on," the first man said, and they fell

onto each other laughing.

When Little T. told Bald Dave, he said, "Son, it don't hurt to be a character. It don't hurt a little bit."

He took Little T. inside his cabin and showed him the material things he had gained from being a character. For anything that people didn't want, they decided Bald Dave might and saved it for him. He had gained a very good alarm clock that way that no one but him had been able to fix; his wife had a whole lot of pretty things on the mantel, vases and carnival dolls and such; he had a slop jar under his bed and a stack of Sears catalogues in his outhouse. He had something everywhere you looked that he wouldn't have had if he had gone around acting as if he were in his right head, he said.

Still, Little T. thought, he had lost something else.

The casting rod had come to Little T. as a hand-me-down. First it had been Mister Jordan Moody's, than Big T.'s. There were few white people even, in these parts, who had a casting rod. And no one had one as fine as this one once had been. While Little T. still worked at the Moodys', Mister Jordan had ordered it from a New York store. It had had many special features, but now the reel leaked grease and creaked as if there were sand in it, despite the many times Little T. had taken it apart and found none. The free spool often did not work right and unwound unexpectedly. Then with the

butt of the rod pushed half through his belly, Little
T. had to try, all at once, to untangle the line, get it
reeled in, keep it from tangling more and keep the
lure unsnagged, which was impossible. In the midst
of everything the reel invariably slipped off the
rod. Then he had the devil's own time juggling the
two pieces, still trying to do everything else. At
these times, he secretly shot envious glances toward everyone else sitting along the bank, their
lines tossed peacefully into the water, their poles
limp in their hands. He usually had to wade into the
water to unsnag his lure; often he had to dive to do
so. Then people along the bank called out, "Hey,
Little T. going to catch that cat one way or another!"

Some people said he would not catch the cat at
all with anything artificial, that he needed a good
bait to drag deep along the bottom of the creek.
But, Little T. said, who had caught her with a good
piece of bait yet? And then what could they say?
This was no ordinary cat, he said. It needed something special.

Little T. and his daddy had seldom supplemented
the fifteen dollars a month by taking odd jobs, and
now Little T. owed money everywhere. His check
was already promised each month before he got it.
The day he had first seen the lure he had ten cents
in his pocket, and even if he had taken that out and
said, "Miss Loma, will you credit this toward the
lure?" she would have said, "Little T., I'm credit-

ing this toward your grocery bill." He knew Miss
Loma. So all he could do that afternoon was stand
there and long. After he had spoken about it, every
man in the store that afternoon had crowded up to
look at the lure. Sooner or later somebody was going to buy it: his lure. Regretfully he had watched
Miss Loma return it to the case. The other things
there that had once seemed so desirable no longer
did. The other lures, the flies, the shiny line, the
reels, the corks all looked old and dusty, as if Miss
Loma had had them for two thousand years.

By the time Little T. reached the bottomland his
breath came cool. He could almost see it before
him. His mission accomplished, he was no longer
afraid. He told himself, and believed it, that the lure
was going to be his. If no one hounded him for
money in the next few weeks, he might save two or
three cents out of the quarter he had made tonight.
There was only one drugstore in Senatobia, and he
could not risk buying the medicine there too many
times.

But he had it in his mind now to work on some
way to get to Memphis. However, he was not sure
how many bottles of medicine Miss Ruth Edna
could buy at once. He had the impression she did
not have money any more readily than he did. That
was one reason he would not have tried to cheat
her, though he knew she did not want anyone to
know about their transactions. And the main reason
was, take any given situation, and the cards were

already stacked against him: she was a woman, and she was white.

Little T.'s motto was, Keep your nose in your own business, keep your mouth shut and keep out of trouble. He intended doing those three things about the two things he had seen tonight.

7

Before the roosters were up next morning, Kate French's brother-in-law, Red Anderson, with Buck French, Homer Brown and Hoyt Springfield, drove off to Whitehill. It was Red's car and he drove. When they got into the car the men closed the doors as softly as possible, not wanting people to hear a car at that hour and slide from bed to peer out. Even so, driving out of town, the two in the back seat watched out the back window for any shades raised out of curiosity. Then they turned and settled down to be borne over the twisted, dipping country road at the abandoned rate of speed of all country drivers. The semi-darkness of the early morning lent itself to the exhilarated feeling of conspiracy the secret meeting had already given them. They did not feel like grown men doing a civic duty, but laughed and joked like boys set free from school. After a long stretch of hot weather that dated back to March, the chill of the early fall morning had caught them by surprise. None of them had dressed warmly enough, and they shivered, believing it was from excitement.

"Look at the trees yonder," Red said, glancing away from the road. "Full turned. Seems like fall's on us all of a sudden."

"Shoot, man, it's near about going to be November," Hoyt said from the back seat. "Christmas'll be on us before we know it."

"Christmas, shit," Buck French said. "I ain't finished paying on last Christmas yet." He rolled down the window and spat out.

"Look a-yonder at the quail rising—over where the sun's coming up," Hoyt said. "Man, I wish I had me a gun. If I wouldn't like to have me some birds and biscuits and gravy."

"You can get 'em soon enough," Homer said. "The weather's getting just cold enough. J. T. Veazey's already got pigeons in his freezer."

"That ain't all he's got in there either," Hoyt said. "He's got enough in there to feed a army the next five years. J. T. don't spend his time doing nothing but hunting."

"He's sluffed all his work off on his boys. He ain't got nothing else to do, why not?" Homer said, thinking how all morning he'd have his sign hung out: No Gas Till Afternoon; losing money.

They gazed for a while over the quiet vista while the sun came up and melted the little frost there had been; the day would be warm and pretty. A

144

white mist rose and slowly dissolved as the sun came full, round and yellow-red. By the time the last few miles were covered, the men were no longer cold. On the outskirts of town, Negroes were just getting up, the smell of wood smoke filled the air, and the smoke itself drifted gray as fog across the road. Into one grassless yard a woman threw a wash basin of gray soapy water and when it splashed, chickens ran to peck in the puddle. In another yard a boy too sleepy to grin drew water from a well. Opposite him a man washing on his front porch pulled up his overalls straps as they passed.

They reached the highway and stopped for a light. Across the road they could see the town. Built on three sides around a square, it was U-shaped as they faced it. Once it had been farther down the highway but had been moved when the highway was straightened. Some of the stores were still the original old white frame buildings, but there were new stores of a pale gold-colored brick. A wooden roof jutted out over the store fronts and shaded the sidewalks and at its farthest curves the U was broken by roads that led away to the houses of the town. Backless wooden benches set against the store fronts lined the sidewalk. There were no townspeople about yet, but one segment of the sidewalk was covered by people separated into two groups, Negroes and whites. They stood near a large truck parked at the curb, and when Red had driven across the highway and into the town, the men could read a large sign propped against one wheel: COTTON PICKERS FOR ARKANSAS. BACK BY SUNDOWN. $1.00 A 100 LBS.

Nearby a man stood and signed people up by writing their names into a black notebook. Then one by one, men and women, Negroes and white, they climbed into the truck and sat together.

"Well, ain't that highjackin'," Hoyt said.

"Shoot, there ain't enough cotton left in this part of Mississippi now to pick," Buck French said. "They got to get together a little chitling money somehow."

"I guess we're kind of early," Homer said. "You reckon the marshal will be at the jail?"

"He will be by eight o'clock," Red said. "We don't have long to wait till then."

They parked in front of the jail at right angles to the sidewalk. The jail was one of the newer yellow-brick buildings, a small two-room affair meant only to hold minor offenders. Other offenders went twenty miles away to Desoto, the county seat, where there was a new and larger red-brick jail and a new brick county courthouse. The men got out of the car and went up and down the sidewalk stretching themselves and looking in at the displays in the store windows. Outside a grocery, Buck French sucked on his teeth and studied a display of Call of the North potatoes from South Dakota; they were in feed sacks from five to fifty pounds. Prices, he

noted, were the same as in Marigold. Homer and
Hoyt studied guns and saddles in a store a few
paces away, but Red went to the end of the block,
his eye attracted by a large printed sign on the post
office. He called, "Hey, you-all come here."

The three others came over and stood with their
hands in their pockets and read:

WARNING

A mad dog was killed in Whitehill on
Tuesday morning, October 15. The Mayor
and Board of Aldermen, town of Whitehill, have ordered all dogs confined for a
period of thirty days beginning October
15. All dogs must be vaccinated immediately. A representative of the Health Department will be in Whitehill on October
16 and 17 from 7 A.M. to 7 P.M.

To vaccinate dogs $1.00.

It is most important that we have your
co-operation.

John Joe Williams, Jr.   Reynold T. Walker
    Mayor   County Health Officer

"I be, I can't remember a mad-dog scare in I
don't know when," Homer said.

A maroon Chevrolet sedan drove slowly past
them and parked before the jail. The driver got out
and went around and opened the car's trunk. He

took out a bird hound and carried the dog into the jail. Then he returned for the dog's puppy and took it inside too.

"I reckon it is open after all," Hoyt said.

The four of them stepped inside the jail to face a room turned into a veterinary station. The health officer, pale and unshaven, about to inject one of the trembling dogs, looked up and indicated the marshal should close the door. He took his feet from his desk and did so; then the men stood before him in the tiny entranceway. The marshal returned to his desk and leaned back in a swivel chair. There was a loud yelp from the back room, and then Red said, "How do. We come to see you about a commitment."

"Not about a dog?" the marshal said, in some surprise. He looked tired too. "I ain't done nothing but dog work for two days. People don't pay no more attention to hours posted on a sign than a dog does hisself. We was here half the night."

"Well it ain't exactly about a dog," Red said, smiling. "It's about Jake Darby."

"Ain't had a peep out of him since he's been here," the marshal said.

Hoyt said, "He can't——" Buck French jabbed him in the ribs.

"You want to see him?" the marshal said.

"No," Red said. "We just want to find out about how to go about committing him. He went out-and-out crazy in Marigold last evening. Ran around in the middle of town just like one of these dogs you folks are scared about. Foaming at the mouth and carrying on. Just plain carrying on. Rushing at folks and crying out. We decided he just ain't safe to have about any more. And he don't have one soul of kin to look after him."

"I thought those folks that brought him last night was his kinfolks," the marshal said.

"Naw," Red said. "He's got a brother somewhere. His Ma died some time ago. Some folks look after him a little, but he stays by hisself."

"Well, it's none of my nevermind," the marshal said. He pulled open a drawer and brought out a white paper form. "You got to go to Desoto to the county courthouse and get this filled out. You see the deputy probate clerk there."

"Much obliged," Red said. He took the paper, folded it and put it into his back pocket.

"You don't want to see him?" the marshal said.

"No," Homer Brown said.

"No," Red said, backing out. "You just keep him here till we do all this, will you?"

"I will if I see fit," the marshal said. "If I get some word from Desoto, I will."

"How long you reckon it's going to take to do this?" Red said, slapping his back pocket.

"Depends," the marshal said.

"Well, much obliged again," Red said. The others mumbled various thanks, and they all went out again gladly into the now bright morning and got into the car. Homer Brown thought, Shoot, it's going to be a whole day's worth of business lost.

They drove down the street to the highway again, but this time turned right. The ride would be a straight little run down the highway for twenty miles to Desoto. The highway went straight on beyond there for some twenty more miles to Memphis. The landscape at first was not much different from that they had traveled in the early morning; the exceptions were a few brick houses set close to the highway as they left Whitehill, and a white filling station gleaming in the sun, fronted by what looked to be one hundred feet of blacktopped drive-in space, which Homer gazed back at with envy. Shortly they passed the pride of the town, a landing field that had been smoothed out of land once furrowed and planted; it was a base for the little light planes that did crop dusting, and flying lessons were given to anyone who wanted them, but no one ever had. There was no hangar, only a slightly built wooden shed where people could come in out of bad weather and where the few records that had to be kept were stored. Landing strips were defined by old automobile tires laid flat on the ground and painted white with a luminous paint. Boundaries were defined in the same way, except that the tires touched one another and stood on end like hoops ready to be rolled. There were no lights. But the planes had flown in successfully late into the evening by the glow of the tires, and the field was considered complete.

Red stopped the car while the four men stared openmouthed as a dot in the distance in the sky took shape as a wobbly little plane coming down: restlessly, like an insect unable to decide where it was going to settle. It seemed to hover and then bounded up again only to come down again, lifted and lowered by the wind. Coming head on, it seemed to be grinning, the whirling propeller was its nose and the two dark windows its eyes. It flew straight ahead over the car, so close they all agreed afterward on the numbers painted beneath the wings.

"Jesus Christ!" Hoyt called. They all threw up their hands and ducked to the floor until they heard the plane fly back over the car and land with a slight thump nearby; then they sat up shamefacedly, grinning at one another and out the windows at the pilot, who was bouncing along grinning and waving at them from the cockpit. Homer and Hoyt, who were sitting on the side by the field, waved back.

"Whew," Red said. They drove on, and along where they drove it looked as if winter had come already; the landscape was dry and brown except for the sudden interruptions of velvety green pines, which grew out of the crumbling roadbanks with their needles shining in the bright white sun the color of stars. In a grove of the pines, like an oasis against the winterscape, sat a great white barn, the hillside leading to it thickly dotted with grazing Black Angus cattle.

"Jordan Moody's," Red said reverently.

Buck French read the lettering over the door of the barn. "Black Angus cattle," he said.

"You ever heard about his auctions?" Hoyt said. "Anybody wants to can come. They come from miles around, interested in buying cattle or no. He passes out free barbecue, potato salad, beer. I don't know what all he don't serve and free as you please to anybody who wants it. They say it's just a big party for the county and more."

"Folks spend the whole day. Some even come from Memphis. Folks bring kids and prac'ly camp out, I hear," Homer said.

"Shoot, if he's feedin' free, they prob'ly bring their grandmammies and daddies and uncles and aunties and anybody else they got," Red said.

"Last year he sold one bull for fifty thousand dollars," Hoyt said.

"Fifty thousand dollars," Red said. "I'd like to see me any bull worth that much."

"It's the truth," Hoyt said. "Some fellow from out West bought it. These cattle people come here from all over."

"I got me a mind to come to the next one," Homer said.

"There was a sign upside the barn that said one in February," Buck said. "I think I might go myself."

152

"I wouldn't mind seeing something walking around on four legs worth fifty thousand dollars," Hoyt said.

"Me either," Red said.

"Crick's dry for this time of year," Hoyt said, looking out as they went over it.

"Look a-yonder, if that ain't a picture," Homer said. Three little Negro girls with blue hula hoops stood by the side of the road, undulating in them. The men waved and the girls waved back, their mouths stretched wide in pleasure and pride.

They saw the water tower in the distance, and Homer put back on his shoes. Buck French threw away the toothpick he had been chewing on and blew his nose. Red figured he still had time for a few good puffs on a cigarette and lit one. Everyone was suddenly thinking of the reason they had come; but if they had ever had any doubts, they had come in the previous short night and had been dispelled at dawn by the relentless, frowzy-haired wives who had been up even before they were, making coffee and starting them on their way. Now they were only thinking of exactly what they would have to do. Red had drawn the paper from his back pocket, and he handed it to Homer. "We ought to look this over," he said.

"First thing," Buck French said, looking at Hoyt, "is you best not say he can't talk, like maybe he's a deaf-and-dumb. They don't take idiots."

"How'd you know that?" Homer said. He had

opened the paper and was reading it.

"I don't know how I knew, I just knew," Buck said. "Don't it say that there?"

"That's exactly what it says," Homer said. "One of us has got to be 'the undersigned'—that is, one of us has got to sign this and state that we suspect Jake of being in-sane, but that he ain't a idiot or feebleminded——"

"Well, ain't that exactly the whole thing," Red said. "We always thought he was a idiot and then he went to actin' up and carryin' on till now we think he's crazy instead. And most likely has been, when you come to think of it, all this time. There's lots of folks that talks that's idiots. Because he don't talk don't necessarily make him a idiot or feeble in his head either."

"I just as soon not say nothing about his not talkin'," Homer said.

"I agree to that," Red said.

The others said they did too.

"Who's going to sign this here saying you suspect him of being in-sane?" Homer said.

Nobody said anything.

"Well, we'll just have to let them folks decide that," Homer said, and read on: "Blank is suspected of being in-sane, is not an idiot or feebleminded; that blank is a poor person—" He looked up. "Well, Jake is shore that," he said. He looked at the paper again and read, "—and has no estate or property except—— What's he got?"

154

"Nothing but that old house that's no more'n a shack now," Buck French said.

"Well, that ain't going to count nothin' in his favor, do you reckon?" Homer said.

"I don't see how it could," Hoyt said.

"Nah," Red said.

Homer said, "Who's ever going to sign this has got to swear Jake don't have anybody legally liable for his maintenance. And he don't have that——"

"Unless somebody knows where Jud's at," Buck French said.

"Well, nobody does know," Homer said. "And I doubt if he could take care of him if they did find him, from whatever I heard about him after he left."

"I heard he done right well," Hoyt said.

"Don't anybody know is the fact," Homer said. "Well, it says he's got to be a citizen of the country and a resident of this state for twelve months and wasn't in-sane when he come into—well, he ain't never been out of, so we don't have to worry. And has been a resident of said county for sixty, then it says six-o in parentheses, days or more and was not—oh well, he ain't ever been out of his own county even. Uh-oh," he said, turning over the page.

The two on the back seat sat forward and Hoyt said, "What?"

"Two doctors got to sign this," Homer said. He looked at the men in the back and then turned and looked at Red, who had taken his eyes off the road to turn and look at him. Then Red looked in the rear-view mirror at the other two. They all thought of the possibility of failure and of their wives. Buck French told himself, Kate'll be up here tomorrow if I don't do it, and somehow she'll get it done.

"They got to be practicing physicians of the county," Homer said. "They got to this day personally examine him and declare about how old he is—well, we can tell 'em about how old he is—that he ain't subject to no contagious diseases—you don't reckon he is, do you?"

"If he is, I don't know where he got 'em, 'less it was from that old cow he used to have," Buck French said, and laughed.

"Or somebody's bitch," Red said.

Everybody laughed.

"And declare," Homer said, "that the in-sanity is of blank duration—what would you say, lifetime, I guess—and that he ain't a idiot or feebleminded —well, we'll just have to trust to luck—and that the medical treatment has been blank, blank, blank. Then in parentheses it says, 'Here set out the medical treatment and all circumstances known to the physician tending to illustrate the same.' You-all understand all that?"

"Not exactly," Hoyt said.

"It's all right," Buck said.

"Then there's a place where the deputy probate

clerk got to sign and the judge of probate court. Whew, we're liable to be here till suppertime," Homer said. "And—" he paused for effect and looked around before he said—"the judge has to appoint a guardian—a suitable and proper person, it says, to act as guardian *a-d* and another word *l-i-t-e-m* for the defendant in this cause. What could those words mean?"

"It's some legal flibbery-gibbery," Buck French said.

"I know that," Homer said.

"You reckon it means a guardian for the rest of his life or something like that?" Red said. "You know ain't none of us going to sign up to do that or anybody else in Marigold."

"Well, let's worry about it when we get there," Buck said.

The courthouse was in the middle of town, set on a square, and the highway led right past it. Red had to slow for a light hung over the road and as they waited for it, an old Ford pick-up crossed before them, a bird dog sitting alertly on the fender. When the light changed, Red pulled from the highway straight into one of the parking places at angles to the square. The square was patchy with grass and was mostly dirt; it was shaded by two magnolia trees so enormous they spread over the entire front of the square. Old men, some with open flies, sat about on benches in the shade.

A black dog carrying a slice of white bread in his mouth looked for a place to eat it; he passed before the men as they entered the cool concrete interior of the building. Brass spittoons lined the corridor and signs were posted, headed in large letters by WARNING or WANTED or FOR SALE. They stopped the first person they met, and Red asked the way to the deputy probate clerk. His office was crowded when they entered it, and they had to stand in line until almost noon waiting their turn. He was a little man sitting behind a large desk, and they told him their story: how Jake had run about and foamed and made the terrible noises; they swore that he was a citizen of the state and county, that they suspected him of being insane, that they did not *think* he was an idiot or feeble-minded, that he was poor, that he had no one legally liable for him, and all the other things that they had to swear to. The deputy probate clerk filled in the blanks as he read along, and then he said, "Which one of you is going to sign this?"

Nobody said anything; they stuck their hands in their pockets and shuffled their feet. The clerk said, "Well?"

"Can more'n one of us sign?" Hoyt said.

"One," the clerk said.

Homer said, "Red, you drove the car, why don't you sign?"

So Red signed. But he told himself all the time he was writing in "William Thomas Anderson," it really wasn't like he was doing it, because since he had been born nobody had ever called him anything but Red, even in the Army.

With a small flourish the clerk signed his own name in the proper blank, then he consulted some papers and a calendar and said, "There's a commitment hearing here tomorrow. Can he be brought in tomorrow?"

"Don't see why not," Buck French said. "He's just sitting in the jail in Whitehill."

"Well, I'd better get word to the marshal there to bring him here today and put him in the jail here. Then I'll be sure he's going to appear tomorrow. Folks are always not turning up when they're supposed to. Now you-all take this down two doors to the sheriff to sign. Next."

They took the paper the two doors and joined the line there. Only now Red held the paper and stood in the line and the others lounged about the door waiting for him. They had come around a corner of the building, and this room was bright with hot October sunshine. Red stared out the window like a schoolboy trapped indoors while others moved about freely. He saw the dog with the bread still in its mouth begin another search of the square. He felt a mosquito bite him on the back of the neck and heard its singing like the steady hum of the voices in the room. Suddenly he was next and he moved up and handed the sheriff his paper. The sheriff chewed his cigar and without looking up read the paper; then he filled in the proper blanks and signed it. He looked up then and said, "You got to get these blanks on the other side filled in by two doctors. Then you got to bring me back this form. Where is this Jake Darby at?"

"In the jail in Whitehill," Red said. "That other clerk said he'd get him brought here today, though."

"Good," the sheriff said. "Then he'll be in my jail this afternoon and I'll see to it he's up before the judge—let me see—Maurice's got him down here for ten A.M. tomorrow."

"About the doctors . . ." Red said.

"Take the form over yonder to Doc Lawrence in that house next to the big sign that says Justice of the Peace. He's retired, but he's still got a license. It'll cost about five dollars."

"Much obliged," Red said.

He joined the others and told them about the five dollars; they were sorry but all agreed it was worth it; they would all chip in. They went outside and followed the sheriff's directions until they came to the house. It still had the doctor's name on a small placard in one window. He opened the door for them and they stood in his hallway and told him what they wanted. Before Red had half finished, the doctor was already nodding in agreement as if he had heard it all before. He had palsy quite badly but managed to write his name, and almost on the line. Then he called to his wife and had her fill in the other blanks certifying to Jake's approximate age, and to the duration of the insanity, and that he had no other contagious diseases and that he was not an idiot or feeble-minded. His wife said, "I declare, there is more folks putting more folks in the state hospital than the law ought to allow. More than they got room for anyhow, I know that much." She looked at them over her glasses as if they ought to be ashamed.

Red said to the doctor, "This boy's back in Whitehill and we want to get all this done today if we can. Is there anybody else could sign this without having to look at him?"

"I'd take it over to the clinic if it 'as me," the doctor said. He pointed the way. "And say that I sent you."

They went straight down his street and around a corner. The clinic was new too, very plain, and of the same light-colored brick as the courthouse. The yard had just been seeded and a Negro who was watering it turned the hose away from them as they passed.

Someone in the clinic signed it. They could not read who. The name was written as illegibly as a prescription. They had simply gone inside and presented the paper to the nurse-receptionist, told her what they wanted, and said that Doctor Lawrence had sent them. She had not been doing anything but buffing her nails when they came in, but she put the buffer down and looked quite annoyed before she took the paper. Without a word she disappeared through a swinging door, and they glimpsed her for a moment going on her quiet heels down a short bare hall. Presently, she returned with the paper signed, looking more cheerful.

"Is there any . . ." Red said.

"No," she said, before he finished, "there's no charge."

They all said they were much obliged and raised their hats. She smiled and watched them as they went out, again buffing her nails.

The sheriff was already late going out to lunch. He took the paper and said, "You got him a guardian?"

"What exactly do those two other words mean?" Homer said.

"What other two words?" the sheriff said.

"A-d . . ." Homer said.

"It just means he's got to have a guardian while the hearing's going on," the sheriff said. "Somebody who's supposed to protect his rights because he ain't fit to do it hisself, else he shouldn't be here. You all tell me now, 'cause I'm fixing to go acrost this square and feed my face."

"Shoot, none of us wants to drive back to Desoto tomorrow," Hoyt said. "Why don't we make somebody else guardian? J. T. was all hot on this, but didn't want to come up today. Let's tell him he has to tomorrow."

"Yeah, put down J. T. Veazey," Red said.

"The judge does it," the sheriff said. "But you tell Brother Veazey to be here at ten o'clock tomorrow or this don't get done."

"So long," Red said.

"Goodbye," the sheriff said. He came out the door after them and locked it. "You boys looking for a little lunch, there's a good café right acrost the square, Bubba's."

"Much obliged," Homer said. "But I reckon we'll get on back home, won't we?" He looked at the others.

"The womenfolks will bust their bustles if we don't get back and tell them what's happened," Buck said.

"There's only one thing I sure wish we could do, though," Homer said.

"What's that?" Red said.

"Get a ice-cream soda at the drugstore," Homer said.

They all agreed it would be too bad to miss this opportunity for one. They walked across the square with the sun falling on them in stipples through the dark shiny leaves of the magnolias. When they came out of the shade to cross the road, it was a surprise when the sun fell on them, one hot glare after the little speckles. At the drugstore the black dog sniffed about the screen door. "Get on out of here, dog," Red said, opening the door. They went inside. The room was dark and cool and stuffy with the odor of medicines and of the refrigerated box that held the ice cream. The ceiling fan was going, but the owner turned it off when they came in. "What can I do for you boys?" he said.

They climbed onto stools at the fountain and said they would have ice-cream sodas, strawberry, all of them. Then they looked around at two girls sitting at a little round table sipping Cokes in glasses full of shaved ice, and they studied the dirty-looking cases with their crepe-paper-lined shelves full of boxes and bottles of things that made women look good and smell pretty. They drank the sodas slowly and then climbed reluctantly from the stools and paid. When they went outside, the heat made the coldness in their stomachs send a pain through their temples and eyeballs. For a moment they felt sick at their stomachs, and then the moment passed. "Ah," Red said.

"You let that dog in," Homer told Hoyt.

Hoyt went back but returned in a moment and said the owner had said it was all right, it was his dog.

They crossed the road and went along the sidewalk in twos to the car. Attached to the windshield wiper was a small white card. "Oh shit," Red said, untying it. "I forgot to put any money in the thing-a-ma-gig." He read the card. "But look," he said. "It's a note that says, 'Welcome Visitor.' Then it goes on to explain what the meter is for and asks that the next time you use it." They got into the car in the same positions in which they had come.

"Now I call that right friendly," Buck said. "This ain't no bad little old town."

"Heck, it's going to be part of Memphis some day, the way Memphis is growing," Red said. "People will be moving to Marigold and driving to Memphis to work."

"I live to see the day," Homer said.

"You'll be in the right business then, Homer," Red said.

"Huh," Homer said. "I'll be ninety-five years old before that ever comes about."

"Naw, I'm telling you," Red said. He backed the car from the curb, turned, waited for the light to finish turning green and then headed down the long straight stretch of highway, straight into the afternoon sun, toward home.

"You know I was just thinking," Buck French said, suddenly. "What nigger's going to cough up a dollar to get his dog vaccinated?"

"What?" Hoyt said.

"That sign that was on the post office in White-hill. It said a dollar to vaccinate your dog," Buck said.

"Shucks, there's plenty white folks ain't going to pay no dollar to get a needle stuck in some mangy dog they own," Red said.

"And there's kids with dogs ain't never going to get 'em vaccinated," Hoyt said. "And there's strays."

"That mad-dog scare's liable to spread right on to Marigold in a week or less," Buck said. "I tell you, if there's one thing I don't want to have truck with it's a rabid dog."

"Lord," Red said, settling down to the drive. "Seems like time you get one thing off your mind, there's something else."

8

The judge sat upright in his black robe and blinked solemnly through steamy bifocals, his eyes enormous and blurred. Idly he drew back his long loose sleeve and wrote in the proper blank on the paper before him: Jake Darby. After it were two printed words: Insanity Suspect. He peered over his glasses at the man.

Four others had gone before him, one a woman he had almost not committed. Standing there, she had looked like any one of the ordinary middle-aged women in his Sunday-school class. Her yellowed white hair was neatly curled and tucked full of heavy black hairpins. She wore a navy-blue crepe dress that he knew in summer had had white piqué collar and cuffs. Now for fall and winter it had multicolored striped taffeta ones. Her navy straw was set squarely forward on her forehead. She had told a long plausible story, familiar to him. In essence, nobody wanted her. Her few remaining relatives were distant and tolerated her at all only because she had a little money they hoped someday to inherit. Certainly he believed that and was about to say, "Petition rejected," when at the saving moment she said, "What's really the matter with them is they're jealous. Perry Como's in love with me."

Now this one, who looked obviously not right.

"Mister Darby," the judge said, leaning forward, "I've read this petition and heard from your guardian the selfsame reasons why you should be committed to the state hospital at Lee. Do you have anything to say in your own behalf?"

The man did not say anything. He did not even look at the judge and the judge could not have said exactly where he was looking. With a vacant stare he looked into a place no one else could see. Perhaps that was what insanity was, the judge thought, and sighed. After thirty years on the bench observing the sane and the supposedly insane, he had given up really trying to draw a line between the two.

He read to himself the first statement on the outline before him: "(1) The said person is insane (not feebleminded or an idiot), being at large is injurious to self and disadvantageous to the community, and should be committed to a hospital." The folks of Mister Darby's town had sworn to this. Who was he, the judge, who had never seen the fellow before, to say that they were wrong? He looked over at the man who had appeared as

168

guardian. He had ceased to chew his gum and looked back at the judge expectantly. This Mister Veazey had said that he had three kids and was afraid to let them run about free in his town any longer.

Sighing, the judge picked up the paper and read aloud: "It is ordered that Jake Darby be declared and is hereby adjudged insane and be committed to the State Hospital, to be treated and dealt with in accordance with the law and regulations of said Institution. If in the future any means shall be available, either as a part of the estate of said insane person, or of any member of his family liable for his maintenance under the law, then, in either of such events, monies advanced by Forrest County shall be repaid to the County, and such insane person shall be and become a private pay patient so long as his means justify that status."

"You don't have to worry about that," J. T. Veazey said.

"What's that?" the judge said, looking up.

"I said, you don't have to worry about that," J. T. said.

"Never mind," the judge said. He read again: "A copy of these proceedings shall be delivered along with said insane person to the superintendent of said Institution." He signed his name wearily and said, "The hearing's over."

J. T. got up. His rear felt cut through to the bone. The proceedings had been long and his chair a hard wooden one with a ridge down the center. He was anxious to move about and to be out of the overheated airless room where the sheriff had continuously smoked cigars. But something kept him lingering, something he wanted to say. To who? he wondered. The sheriff, the judge, Jake? Yes, Jake, he thought. He walked over to where Jake stood, his shirt soaked through with sweat. He turned and looked at J. T. as he walked up, and already there was something different in his eyes. He stared as if J. T. were a stranger. "Jake," J. T. said. "Don't you know me, boy?"

Jake made no sign.

J. T. wanted to say he was sorry. He opened his mouth to do so, and suddenly he said to himself, Well, I'll be a God-damned son of a bitch.

Tears swelled up and overran his eyes. He pressed Jake's arm and said, "Take care of yourself, boy."

Then he turned and hurried out of the room, down the short corridor and out into the day. The temperature had dropped overnight and the season become the near-winter it was. The warm spell was over. J. T. went to his car and got in and turned on the heater. He drove off shivering and sobbing and snuffling his nose, wiping his eyes so he could see how to drive. Turning onto the highway, he said aloud, "Jesus Christ, old man. I'm glad nobody else come with you."

9

They were all moving about him now, people going in every direction. He stood still and presently, as he had known someone would, a man took his elbow and began to guide him. He stood in a group then, while people came and went, and occasionally he glanced their way. He had not slept for a long time, not since the time they had put him in a room he could not get out of, with many dogs coming and going beyond the bars that confined him. People, standing close, had talked to him off and on, peering, talking as if they had expected him to answer. He could only turn away. He was afraid with strangers to make any sound, and he could not understand why these had expected so much of him.

The old man whose black clothes flowed about him, nipping at his heels as he walked, passed close and said, "Somebody ought to get him a haircut."

"He'll get one when he gets there," another man said.

He was led again by the elbow out into the sweet day, where a wash of cool wind chilled him. Past thin sunlight, beyond the square of ground where people walked briskly, he saw the building he had come out of this early morning; the bars that had bound him at the other place had bound him here too, at the windows and at the door. They were not taking him back there. He moved with the group still, the woman, the three men.

"Perry," said the woman once. "Wait for me."

In his whole life, he had not been in a car as much as he had been these last two days since he had been taken from home. Home. Above all things, he knew he had been taken from home.

Now he was in a car again, sitting straight, not moving, not looking back. He was afraid. They took him through the blue day, past shedding trees and white sunshine, on and on until he saw land such as he had never seen before rising away to a great height and falling back again: he knew he was a long way from home.

Home.

They stopped at gas stations and he looked for Homer Brown, but he was never there. They took him inside into smaller rooms than he had ever been in in his life and told him to go to the bathroom and he did, behind their turned backs. Once they gave him a sandwich and a glass of milk and when he had eaten they said, "Cake?"

He shook his head. He knew the word still: cake. Other voices and other faces, familiar to him, had said it and he had eaten it gladly. Now his stomach did not want even what he had already eaten. All he wanted was to cry.

"I wish they were all good as him," said the man driving; he jerked his head toward Jake.

"Yeah, he's a good one," said his helper.

The others, the three men, the woman, chattered like sparrows around him. One man, next to him, said quite comfortably, "You'd never think this was the last day of the world, would you?"

Then they began to go to sleep, nodding their heads forward, leaning against the sides of the car. But sleep was something he could not remember. He did not know how long it was since he had slept, since he had been away from home. He only knew that the last time he had it had been in his own bed. In the new places he had lain with his eyes open, knowing first that it was morning and then that it was evening and that it was all the same: time made no difference to him.

Only that first morning, in the first place, he had looked up to see Wilroy and Mary Margaret looking in at him. Wilroy had said, "But didn't you even ask 'em their names? Don't you know who they were? Just four men . . ."

And Mary Margaret said, "Just like that. Is it that easy to commit somebody to the insane asylum?"

The marshal said, "All I know is I got a call from Desoto to bring him there, and I ain't doing otherwise. I can't turn him loose."

They had gone away, with Mary Margaret crying; and then Jake had cried too, turning away so that no one could see him. Behind the closed door the dogs had gone on one by one, yelping in pain, and he had chewed his knuckles until they bled, listening. Afterward he had been put into a car and driven off to a place almost the same, bigger, without the dogs. And he had stayed until they took him into the room full of people. And now he was in a car again, going a long way.

The man who helped the driver said restlessly, "Still a ways to go."

"You wanna drive?" the driver said. He pulled to the side of the road and the first man got into the driver's seat. People woke up and yawned and said:

"Are we here?"

"What time is it?"

"Where are we?"

"How much further?"

The car was a station wagon with two upright stiff seats behind the driver's seat. Everyone shuffled about changing places; then everyone went back to sleep again. Only Jake did not move; only he did not sleep. The others had ceased talking to him; they thought he wanted to be alone.

He thought about the wind that had come cold

when he was outside. It was evening, and he thought about that. There was a piece of moon already in the sky and one faint star. He was very tired and would have lured sleep if he had known how.

They arrived when evening deepened. The car followed a long driveway that swept toward a group of lighted buildings; they stopped beneath an archway, though the driveway went on and returned to the highway again. They had not seen anything for a long time but entanglements of weeds along the road and had heard only the insect sounds of night and nothing more. Now the driver said, "Here we are, folks."

Everyone sat up to look out and one of the men, named Charlie, said, "I'm sure glad to be back here with indoor toilets instead of at home."

"Charlie, you always do manage to get back, don't you?" said the driver. "Reckon how long they'll keep you this time?"

"A long time, maybe," Charlie said. "I'm a whole lots crazier than I was the last time."

They told Jake to get out of the car, and he did. He stood beneath the shelter of the archway to look about. As far as he could see there was the flat open lawn with many tall trees stretching away to the highway in the distance, which he could see only when cars, with their yellow lights, went by making a dulled sound of *whoosh*. There were round and square places in the ground where the earth had been worked and flowers grew out of them in neat clumps. Hedges were clipped round as balls and were taller than his head. It did not seem entirely alien, but it was not the same. Almost while he watched, evening disappeared and night came; then it was dark and he could see nothing but lighted windows, the outlines of trees and a lighted doorway behind him. A man came out of the door and down the few steps, welcoming them. In the soft light from the crystal chandelier his steel-rimmed glasses glinted on his nose, his white hair shone as silvery as fish scales, luminous in the night.

"Well, I see you got here all right," he said. He shook hands with the driver and his helper.

"Do they have television here?" the woman whispered to Charlie.

"Oh, sure," Charlie said. "They got everything. Especially if you get sent to the new building. You ought to hope to get sent to the new building."

The doctor turned and said, "Is that you, Charlie? You back again?" He laughed.

"Yes, sir, Doctor," Charlie said happily. "Right back where I started from. Reckon I might as well stay this time."

"Well, we'll see," the doctor said. "You got to make room for others, you know."

The drivers had taken all of the suitcases out of the car and lined them up along the steps. One of them put a shoe box into Jake's arms, and Jake held it fast. "That's all he's got," the man said to the doctor. "Fellow brought it to the court today."

"I see, that's fine," the doctor said. He patted Jake's arm. "We'll all get assigned to our rooms now, and then get cleaned up and have some supper." He herded them toward the stairs. A tall good-looking blond boy came down to them at that moment and began picking up the luggage. "Well, you look like somebody I've seen before," he said to Charlie. "How're you doing? You owe me two dollars from way back on the Yankees."

"Boy, you wouldn't take money from a old crazy man, would you?" Charlie said. He picked up his own suitcase and the two went up the stairs together. At the top Charlie opened the door, turned and said, "Come on in, everybody."

The driver shook his head and said, "Every time I see that blond kid I just can't get over it. He looks and acts just like every kid his age I know hanging around the drugstore at home."

"He's as disturbed as they come, though," the doctor said. "Violent sometimes. But he'll get better."

"I swear it beats all," the man said. "You never can tell." The two men got back into the car and one said, "Well, so long, Doc. See you in another few days." They drove away.

Jake watched the two little red lights disappear into the darkness and then the man next to him said kindly, "Come inside, sir."

A colored woman came down the steps past them. She picked up the rest of the luggage and carried it upstairs. "That's Addie," Charlie said, from the doorway. "She's been here since nineteen and thirty-five."

"We couldn't get along without Addie," the doctor said. He turned to her. "Could we, Addie?" To the others he said, "She cleans our laboratory as clean as any hospital's. It's her special job, and she takes pride in it."

Addie smiled and put down the luggage and went away. A receptionist checked their names against some cards in her hand and pinned little tags on them with their names and room numbers. "Are you Mister Darby?" she said. Jake looked down into eyes as brown as any dog's, with specks of yellow in them like sunlight.

"He ain't said a word the whole way," one of the men said.

"Well, it must be Mister Darby," she said, and pinned the cardboard to him.

Charlie came up close, squinted, and read. "Dad burn it," he said. "You're in the new building. I'm not."

"Am I, am I?" the woman said, jumping up and down with little hops, clapping her hands.

Charlie came close and said, "Yep." No one else was. Charlie said to himself aloud, "Oh, well. Better luck next time."

They took the others away. Charlie called back

178

to the woman and Jake, "See you later."

The woman said, "'Perry Como's on tomorrow. Watch and see what he sings to me."

The receptionist smiled and said, "He's very good-looking."

"*Yes, he is,*" the woman said.

The doctor said, "Come along, Miss Turley, Mister Darby. We have to go outside and across the way to the new building." As they went out the door he said, "You're really the envy of the other patients. We just finished our new building this year. A one-million-dollar building. I bet there's not another finer in any part of the country. I'm sure others think we southern backwoods folks are way behind the times. But we're coming along, I'm here to tell you. We're making progress. There is fine work going on here. You'll see. You'll be like Charlie. You'll want to keep coming back to see us, everything is so nice."

"Oh, no," Miss Turley said. "I have to go to New York next week to meet somebody very special."

"Oh, I see," the doctor said. "What about you, Mister Darby? Do you think you're going to like it here with us?"

"He ain't said a word this whole day," Miss Turley said. She lowered her voice and whispered, "Personally, I don't think he can talk."

"Oh," the doctor said. "I see."

They took Miss Turley into a room full of glass

where a nurse sat at a desk. Beyond the room of glass was another room of glass, with night at the windows. Great leafy plants in large white pots were set about on the floor. There was a television set, and comfortable wicker lounge chairs were drawn up before it. And there were several wheel chairs into which old women were tied by bed-sheets about their waists.

"Television!" Miss Turley said.

"Mrs. Brown, this is Miss Turley," the doctor said to the nurse.

Mrs. Brown got up and walked over and smoothed back a wisp of hair from Miss Turley's forehead. "We're so glad to see you, Miss Turley," she said. "We've got your room all ready. A nice pink one. Do you like pink?"

"I love it," Miss Turley said. "But I'm not staying long. I have to go to New York."

"I always have wanted to go to New York," Mrs. Brown said. She took Miss Turley's suitcase from the doctor and said, "Come along and I'll show you your room. Almost everybody is at a magician's show and they'll go straight from there to supper."

The old women, from their chairs, darted side-long secretive glances after them. Then they bent their noses to their work again—they were all doing some kind of handiwork: knitting, crochet-ing, darning. Occasionally they peeped out from beneath their eyebrows at the television program, as if it were a forbidden pleasure. Or perhaps as if they wished that it were: something covert; something of their own.

One old woman began to claw after her long cotton stockings, which looked as if they had deflated; they had fallen below her knees. A young woman got up from a soft ottoman she had been sitting on, knelt before the woman and rolled the stockings back up. She smiled up at the old woman gently then, and returned to her seat. The old woman looked down at her work and crocheted viciously, smiling in a pleased way.

"I don't know what we'd do if the younger patients didn't help out with the older ones, Mister Darby," said the doctor, who was watching. "We're so understaffed, that's the whole problem, we're so understaffed. Well, come along, we'll go to the men's ward."

They went out of the glass room and into the narrow hall that led between the oblong little rooms all painted pretty pastels: pink, blue, yellow, green. Each had a small bed, bedside table and chest of drawers; the rooms were bare but neat, livened by the colors; each had a small window too high to see out of. In one room Miss Turley was hanging up her dresses, talking excitedly to the nurse. The nurse waved as the doctor and Jake passed.

They passed another room where a pretty young woman sat, her hair nicely waved, her mouth and cheeks nicely rouged. The doctor stood in the door and said, "Didn't you want to see the magic show, Betty Ruth? Or TV?"

"I'm too nervous," the young woman said. "I'm just too nervous, and my eyes hurt me so. That's when my husband knew something was happening to me again, when I got so nervous, and he brought me back here."

"Well, you'll get better again," the doctor said. "And maybe this time you can go home and stay."

"I hope so," she said. "I have two little children, you know. It's so hard to leave them."

"I know it is," the doctor said. "I'll talk to you about it tomorrow."

Outside their rooms two other young women sat slump-shouldered in straight little cane chairs, hands folded in their laps, eyes staring at nothing, not seeming to need to. The doctor stopped by the first, put his hand on her shoulder a moment, and said, "Don't you want to see TV, Miss Davis?"

She looked up at him in an apologetic sort of way and shook her head. "I'm just too nervous, Doc Rutledge," she said. "I just can't look at anything too long."

They passed on to the next girl and the doctor asked her the same question. She looked down into her lap and shook her head from side to side. "No," she said quietly, "my eyes just hurt me too bad. They just jump all over. I can't do anything."

Whenever the doctor had stopped, Jake had stopped, and when he went on, Jake did. Now they passed out between swinging doors into the pink-marble corridor that circled the entire building. On one side the corridor was entirely glass, broken at intervals by closed doors, and looked out onto a grassy patio. The corridor was bare except at intervals where there were recesses with a group of chairs; here patients might see their visitors. As they passed one closed door, the doctor indicated it and said, "That's where you'll have your haircut Monday, Mister Darby. We have a complete barber shop. Three chairs."

Jake looked after his finger and saw a door. Attached to it was something, swirling with color, going around and around.

Outside the door to the men's ward, the doctor suddenly stopped and said, "Mister Darby. Can you talk?"

Talk, Jake heard. He brought his hand to his throat and held it there. He felt tears inside him, and then on his cheeks.

"Never mind," the doctor said. He patted Jake's arm. "If you can't talk, you don't belong here and you won't have to stay."

He pushed open swinging doors. They went into a room like the one they had left except that it was a young man who sat at the desk. He wore a starched white jacket, stiff as a board, and white pants. He stood up and said, "How you, Doc?"

"Sam, this is Mister Darby," the doctor said. "Another ringer, I believe, Sam."

"Is that right?" Sam said. He looked closely at Jake and shrugged his shoulders. "Hard to tell yet."

"Oh, we'll have to keep him the month for observation," the doctor said. "Did Smitty leave today?"

"Yeah, thank God," Sam said. "I can take anything else as long as no more alcoholics get slipped in. They're the worst."

"Everybody go to the magic show?" the doctor said.

"Just about," Sam said. "A few wouldn't go. I'll take this one along and get him ready for supper. That all his things in that box?"

"Yes," the doctor said.

"Jesus," Sam said.

He tried to take the box, but Jake held onto it. Sam let it go. He took Jake by the arm and led him down the hall. The doctor followed to the door of Jake's room. Out of the doorway opposite came an old man, spry as a cricket, who said, "I'm going home today, Doc."

"Is that right?" the doctor said. He looked into the old man's room at the neat piles of his clothes set out on the bed. A suit on a coat hanger was hooked onto a chair. The doctor glanced at Sam and Sam shook his head.

"Well, that's fine," the doctor said. He turned back to Jake. "Have a good supper and a good night's sleep, Mister Darby," he said. "Sam, give him something if he doesn't sleep. He looks tired."

Sam had opened the shoe box and he said, "Here's a note in the box. Can he read?"

"Oh, I doubt it," the doctor said.

"It says to tell him Wilroy and Mary Margaret will be up to see him first time they can," Sam said. "That makes it a week from tomorrow. Visiting day's the first Sunday of every month. It don't seem to be making no big impression on him."

"I told you, I think they slipped one in on us," the doctor said. "I don't believe he can understand even as much as half of what's said to him. We'll see. Whew, I'm tired." He turned away, back down the hall.

"I got some reports up here I'd like you to see a minute if you got time," Sam said.

Then he was gone too. Jake sat down on the bed and looked at his other pair of socks in the shoe box. Gradually he took everything out: a shirt, a change of underwear, a toothbrush and paste, a razor and shaving cream. He took out a little package wrapped in waxed paper and opened it. There was a fried chicken leg, a stuffed egg, and a piece of marble cake. He ate them all. He was licking his fingers when Sam came back. "Uh-oh," Sam said. "You can't have that." He took the razor.

He took Jake into the bathroom and helped him to wash. When they came again into the hall, he called, "Supper, Mister O'Brien!"

Mr. O'Brien popped out of his room on his

little bowed cricket legs, rubbing a round place on his stomach, and said, "It's about time."

They passed a room in which an old man lay sprawled on his bed, one leg trailing on the floor, as if he had lunged at sleep and caught it before he had meant to. Sam shook him hard and woke him, but he came awake reluctantly and grumbled all the way to the dining room.

When they entered the dining room, they were met by the smells of so many different kinds of food, it was as if it were one smell of something unnamable. There were no women in the room, only men, and they sat at long tables, side by side, with attendants at the head. As soon as they sat down someone put plates of food in front of them, and Jake ate what was before him, as the others were doing. When he had finished, the plate was taken away. Then he had ice cream, one round scoop of vanilla, and he ate that. Across from him a man with a day's growth of beard and eyes as pink as a rabbit's leaned forward and said, "Did you know all the waiters are patients too? I hope to be one someday."

"He don't understand," Sam said. "I don't think."

"Oh?" the man said. He turned to the others and said, "Shall we see television after supper?"

"Sure," Sam said, scraping back his chair. "Everybody finished? Let's go."

All around the room was the same sound, the

scraping back of chairs; as the men filed out of the room, two by two, ushered by the attendants, there was the clatter of silverware being thrown onto trays and the clunking sound of heavy plates and mugs being stacked. No one could talk above the noise and the men moved silently until they were some distance down the hall. Then the man walking along beside Jake said, "Did you see him make that long row of scarves come out of that hat when all we had seen him put in it was that little bitty Confederate flag?"

When Jake did not answer or even look at him, he looked at Sam, nodded his head toward Jake, and said, "What's with him?"

Sam shrugged and said, "Cat's got his tongue."

They went back into the ward, and Sam led Jake to a chair in front of the television. When the program had been agreed upon and the machine turned on, he watched to see what Jake did. He merely stared. Presently he began to rub his eyes, fighting their closing. Then as he began to remember sleep, he let himself find it again. He remembered it: the quiet, and the gentle breathing, the dark and then the light. Sam took him by the arm gently and led him away to bed. He helped him to undress. He turned off the light and said from the door, "I'll look in in a little while. If you aren't asleep, I'll give you something."

He lay straight and flat and watched where the light had been. He scratched after the fleas that had been hopping on him ever since he had been in the jail. He listened to the faraway faint sound of a man's voice calling, "Help. Help. Help." It went on for a long time, without urgency.

The box was on a chair beside the bed. Slowly, into the dark, his hand went out until he was touching it. His other socks were still there; he felt them, rolled together. His fingers continued to seek and finally touched the little piece of crumpled paper; he curled his fingers about it and brought it up to himself. He thought how it would be if he could read it. Wilroy, the man had said, looking at it: Mary Margaret. Jake held it to himself a long time smelling only its paper smell; then he put the paper under his pillow and thought of sleep again and let it come again as once he had known it, trusting it, believing in it, believing that tomorrow everything would be the same again.

10

The bus stop for Lee was also a grocery store. Alighting from the bus, Wilroy and Mary Margaret went inside and asked directions to the hospital. The owner's wife sat by the front window on a raised platform at a very high old wooden desk and kept grocery accounts, gave out information about the bus schedule and sold tickets. She looked down and said, "You passed it coming in. You could have rung and got off there."

"Oh, well, we didn't know," Wilroy said. "How we going to get back there?"

"You can take a taxi is all," the woman said, pointing her pencil. "There's the stand right over there."

Looking through the window, Wilroy and Mary Margaret saw the current prices of vegetables backwards, painted on the window in blue poster paint, and across the street to a one-room wooden shed with a sign on the roof: TAXI. Beside the shed an old Plymouth and an old Chevrolet were drawn up. On a bench two men sat talking in the late October sun.

"I told you I thought all those buildings we passed must have been the hospital," Mary Margaret said.

"I didn't see no sign," Wilroy said.

"There was one," the woman said.

"What's the chances on us gettin' back to Marigold this evening?" Wilroy said.

The woman consulted a schedule. "Bus at four o'clock will get you in at ten. Otherwise you're going to arrive back in the middle of the night."

"We'll have to make that one, then." Wilroy looked at Mary Margaret, and she nodded.

"Bus station closes up at one o'clock Sundays," the woman said. "Just flag the bus down outside the hospital. You want a ticket now?"

"Got one! Round trip." Wilroy slapped his breast pocket proudly, took Mary Margaret's arm and guided her away from the bin full of sale items, out of the store and across the street. "They don't sell nothing on Sundays. The store's just open for the bus station."

"Well, I wondered. I never had heard even of a grocery in Memphis being open on Sunday."

Approaching the men, Wilroy said, "We'd like to go out to the hospital, please, sir."

One man, his mouth widening like a yawning animal's, shouted, "*Ag*—nes!"

When his wife appeared wearing an old sea

captain's hat, he said, "These folks want to go out to the hospital."

Without a word Agnes got into the Plymouth; Wilroy and Mary Margaret got into the back. Mary Margaret put her hand on Wilroy's knee a moment. They felt quite romantic, quite excited about this little trip. It was the first they had ever taken that Wilroy did not do the driving. But they had been won over by the bus company's television commercial: *You'll see more from a bus be-cause the dri-ving's up to us!* De, da, the tune went through Mary Margaret's head still, quite catchy.

But their bus had not been the luxurious two-decker with the glass bubble dome that on television rolled smoothly past the Grand Canyon and the giant redwoods of California. It had been the same old carbon-monoxide kind, with one level of two rows of double seats, that they had always known. Their disappointment had not dampened their spirits; they gazed about eagerly at everything. To tell the truth, Mary Margaret did not find Lee as pretty as Senatobia despite rolling hills in the distance, though she would not have said so for fear of offending the woman.

"How're you folks?" Agnes said.

"Doing all right," Wilroy said. "How you doing?"

"Fine." Agnes drove the car on rapidly and suddenly swerved to the side of the road and stopped.

"Hey, Billy! You got some greens?"

On the opposite side of the road an old man in khaki work clothes and a red-plaid hunting cap was walking, head bent, toward town. He looked up in surprise. "Yes 'um. Can you use some?"

"I been looking all over for some."

Billy crossed the road and handed her through the window a stuffed paper grocery sack.

"How much you want for 'em?"

"Quarter do?"

Agnes gave him a quarter and drove off rapidly, blaring the horn at an incautious chicken.

"Did he sell all those greens for a quarter!" Mary Margaret said.

"Oh, he's one of the patients out to the hospital. He thinks a quarter's a lot of money."

"One of the patients! They let them run free like that?"

"When they been there a long time. Billy's been there thirty years. He was going in to sell his greens. He'd sell 'em for the same in town. He might as well sell 'em to me."

"Where'd he get the greens?" Wilroy said.

"They give 'em a little garden. And the patients take care of the hospital's garden. That's most likely where he got 'em. They had a big to-do for a while. The superintendent said he was going to stop 'em all taking things and selling 'em in town. But he never did anything."

She turned in abruptly between two brick posts.

"Which building you want?"

"Administration, I believe," Wilroy said.

When Agnes stopped, he paid her the dollar she asked for, and they all said goodbye. Then he and Mary Margaret stood beneath the great stone archway and looked at each other in surprise. "I declare to my soul, Wilroy," Mary Margaret said. "I never expected anything like this. I thought it would be all dark and drab and dingy, like a prison, you know."

Surprised himself, Wilroy said nothing. He took Mary Margaret's arm, and they went inside the building. It was an old mansion. Overhead on a fine chain a crystal chandelier hung with its prisms reflecting one another, sparkling, glistening, full of a rainbow's colors, like raindrops after the sun has come out. On either side of the room a staircase curved up gracefully to form one suspended overhead, shutting out most of the light from a large stained-glass window close to the ceiling. The gloom gave a hush to the room. Wilroy spoke softly when he asked directions to Jake's doctor. The receptionist smiled and directed them to the new building, on their left as they came in.

When they went out again, Mary Margaret glanced about self-consciously, wondering if anyone would think they were new patients. It was hard to tell who belonged and who didn't; somehow she had thought the people would look different.

They passed a waist-high red brick wall and looked over it at a formal garden. Espaliered against the wall were ivy and pyracantha in designs intricate as a spider's web. In each corner stood concrete urns, goblet-shaped, full of rich dark earth and the last of miniature roses and violets. Into the garden, stepping on slabs of marble shiny as ice, came an old man wearing a hat squashed onto his head like a saucer. He bent to the chrysanthemums, mumbling to himself, then straightened and throwing his arms heavenward cried, "In the beginning . . . !"

Embarrassed, Wilroy and Mary Margaret tiptoed away. They looked back only once, and the old man was still delivering his sermon. The sidewalk led past barred windows, and women standing behind dark screens looked out at them silently. In the men's wing a faceless voice said, "Hello, honey."

Taking Mary Margaret's arm, Wilroy hurried them on faster. Mary Margaret felt herself flush in a funny way, as if it were her fault the man called out. Perhaps it was that she felt guilty: she was on the outside, and he was not.

"Did you hear a man calling 'help'?" she said, in a whisper.

"I thought I did, but then I decided it couldn't have been."

"It was. But it was as if he didn't really mean it."

"You reckon there's going to be a place here where we can eat?" Wilroy said. "I'm starving."

"Lord, I hope so." Mary Margaret, on a diet, had eaten only cottage cheese for breakfast. An irrepressible desire for something sweet had overtaken her. Unable to suppress it, she had gone on, actually, to deciding between a milk shake and a sundae.

Wilroy pushed open glass doors, and they entered a foyer of pink marble. At its opposite end a glass wall looked onto a patio where patients sat at small round tables gay with beach umbrellas. A receptionist showed them down the hall to Doctor Rutledge's door.

He rose when they entered, a short, somewhat round man who peered at them closely. Then Mary Margaret noticed his glasses swinging in his hand; on either side of his nose was a depressed red mark. They introduced themselves and sat down. Wilroy said, "Well, how's our boy?"

"To tell the truth, we've had some trouble with him," the doctor said. "In the barbershop mainly. I looked at his record and believe his behavior must be about the same as when you decided to commit him here."

"It wasn't none of us," Wilroy said, quickly. "It was some folks in the town that never had taken a particular tuck to Jake anyhow."

"He's never been to a barbershop," Mary Margaret said. "If you took him to town to a real one."

"Well, the barbershop's here. But it's real."
The doctor smiled. "I'll tell you. Mr. Darby's at
lunch and until he finishes we could take a little
walk around. I'd like to show you our building
and tell you something of our work here. And I'd
like to talk to you about Mr. Darby."

They rose and went into the hall. The doctor
pointed to the patio as they passed it. "Notice our
building is built in an unbroken circle around that
patio. The patients can sit there with a feeling of
complete freedom. Yet no one can leave it without
being seen."

"Well, I declare. I call that smart," Wilroy
said.

"How did Mr. Darby get his hair cut?" the
doctor said.

"Wilroy did it, or a colored woman that use to
come help him out, and a friend of mine, Miss
May," Mary Margaret said. "But they just used
scissors."

"He was probably afraid of the electric clip-
pers," the doctor said. "Of course that's what's
been so hard. Not knowing what he knows and
what he doesn't."

"Well, that's always been the case," Mary Margaret said. "But some friends of mine and I—
Loma and Ruth Edna, Wilroy—believe sometimes
he knows more than we do."

"If it was anybody but you three women I'd
take issue with that." Wilroy winked at the doctor.

"Now, Wilroy——," Mary Margaret said.

The doctor said, "Look here." They stopped outside the barbershop, which was locked because it was Sunday. The doctor unlocked the door and they stepped inside.

"Well now, this ain't no bad apples," Wilroy said.

When they had inspected everything, they went again into the hall. The doctor stopped outside a pink door and said to Mary Margaret, "This is for you." He unlocked the door and she went past him. "Why, Doctor Rutledge, I declare to my soul. If this isn't something to tell them back home, Wilroy. A beauty parlor, and better than anything we got between home and Memphis, too." She studied the aqua walls and the pale-pink chairs and the coffee table laden with fashion and movie and homemaking magazines.

The doctor said, "Of course, all of our patients are poor. They've seldom been to barbers or beauty shops. But then, a lot of them have never slept in a bed to themselves or had indoor toilets or enough good food before, either. That's why a lot of them had rather be here than at home."

"I can imagine," Mary Margaret said.

The doctor closed the door. They continued down the hall. "A lot of our women patients are just housewives who can't handle all their responsibilities. They don't have enough money and too many kids. The father might be unable to provide, or unwilling, or perhaps drinks. Given a whole set of other circumstances, they probably would never have had any trouble. What's done for them in the beauty parlor probably helps as much as what we doctors do."

He and Wilroy had gotten ahead. Now Wilroy was asking about a place to eat lunch. Lagging behind, Mary Margaret could not stop thinking about those women, poor souls. She sometimes had thought she wasn't going to get through any given day, what with the housework and the gardening and the kids when they were small. If you didn't have a strong man beside you, as she had Wilroy, what would you do? She'd never realized before it was nervous breakdowns that sent folks here. She'd always thought that when you got locked up you were just plain nuts, off forever. Though here you didn't feel you were locked up. That's what the doctor had said they were striving for. Two years ago they had torn down the high brick fence that once enclosed the place. She wondered what the women thought about under the dryer when they couldn't talk to anybody, and nobody could talk to them, and there was nothing else for your mind to run to but thinking? The idea that the women in this place were concerned with how to get their hair fixed brought a lump to her throat.

When she reached Wilroy and the doctor, the doctor said, "I was going to show you the swimming pool and the gym, but the time's getting short. And your husband says you folks want a bite, so I'll show you to the snack shop. Afterward you can pick Mr. Darby up in his ward and visit in one of the recesses we've passed in the hall, where there are nice comfortable chairs and couches."

"I hate to miss the pool," Wilroy said. "But my stomach's just a-growling. I smell food."

The doctor laughed. "It's right around the corner. Perhaps you can see the pool later. It's beautiful. Almost Olympic size. The water blue as a robin's egg. The gym has a basketball court, and the patients play the town team. We've got every kind of exercising thing you can think of. Tumbling mats, boxing gloves, stationary bicycles. And there's a crafts shop, too. The patients can do metalwork, quilting, painting, carpentry, and there's even a loom."

"I hope we can see some of those things later," Wilroy said. "Though we got to get a four o'clock bus."

"Remember where I told you you could pick up Mr. Darby?" the doctor said. He put out his hand and met Wilroy's. They shook hard, then let go. "I just want to tell you one more thing, then I'll let you eat. That is, I don't believe Mr. Darby belongs here."

"Oh?" Mary Margaret said. "Then is he coming home?"

"Most likely. But not before a month is up. We have to keep everybody committed here a month for observation."

"That seems too bad," Wilroy said, "if you don't think they belong."

"It is, because it fosters our worst problem, over-crowding. We get many people who don't belong here. Alcoholics mainly. Families who can't afford to send them to private institutions, or don't want to bother with them, send them here. Then they get a rest from them for a month, and the patient gets a free cure."

"How do they get 'em in?" Wilroy said.

"Same way your friend was gotten in. The family goes to court and swears them to be insane. There aren't enough caseworkers to go into the cases thoroughly. It's a very underpaid job. The courts don't pay enough attention either, and there are always doctors who are friends of the family or who'll take a fee for signing the petition. After all, if the person's going to be released in a month, what's the harm—except to the state. The case-workers don't have the right facilities either. It's common practice to keep people in jail waiting to be committed. Sometimes that can be a week or two. You can imagine the influences they come under there." He smiled a little. "Mr. Darby was covered with fleas."

"Oh." Mary Margaret's hand flew to her mouth.

"Mr. Darby has an aphasia, a loss of speech. Evidently he's had it from birth. I am certain he cannot be cured, and I don't believe he can be helped here. We can't take people we can't help. There's too many we can."

"Then he is coming home," Mary Margaret said.

"I feel pretty sure," the doctor said.

"Say, don't any of these folks you let just walk around free ever just keep going?" Wilroy said. They had rounded the corner, and he saw the snack shop ahead.

"Occasionally. But we find them and bring them back. We have more trouble with families taking them off. They get to feeling guilty or decide the person is well, come to take them for a drive and keep on going. Or if the patient goes home for a visit, the family doesn't bother to bring him back. All we can do is notify the court nearest them, and if they can't get the person sent back, then that's the end of it." He poked his head inside the shop. "Alice, take care of these folks."

A pleasant-looking woman behind the counter said, "I sure will, Doc."

"Alice is a patient," the doctor whispered to Mary Margaret. "She's been helping out in here for twenty years." He shook hands again and went off down the hall.

Mary Margaret sat at the counter as close as she could to Wilroy. She wished she could get over the feeling that at any moment a patient might draw out a knife and stick her in the back. She passed up a dieter's vegetable plate and joined Wilroy in a hamburger and chocolate milk shake.

Just as they finished, a man in a white uniform entered and said to the young man who had been sitting beside her the whole time, drinking a Coke, "Are you finished? Was it good?"

The young man got up and smiled, somewhat sadly Mary Margaret thought, before he left. Her heart went out to him, but her blood ran cold.

When they went to Jake's ward, she asked the young man at the desk, "Will our friend have to have a warden with him while he's talking to us?"

"Warden!" The young man almost jumped from his chair. "We're not wardens. We're called attendants, or preferably psychiatric aides."

"Oh, I'm so sorry," Mary Margaret said, and the young man said, "Oh, it's all right. You're not the first," but Mary Margaret felt his eyes on her as she and Wilroy pushed through swinging doors into the television room, as he had directed. They stood close together and looked about. There were men looking at the set, or playing cards at a table in one corner, or just sitting. Over by the window, in the sunshine, Jake sat on a narrow chair, his knees pulled up close, looking at the floor.

They approached him slowly, not wanting to scare him, preparing themselves. They stood right in front of him before he looked up. "Jake, honey," Mary Margaret said, softly. "It's us."

Tears slowly filled his eyes. One hand started toward them involuntarily and then clutched his knee instead. Mary Margaret reached down for it, groping because her own eyes were blinded by tears. Even Wilroy had to blow his nose. "Let's take him out in the hall, like the doctor said," he said. He bent over and took Jake's elbow, and Jake got up. Mary Margaret took his other elbow, and between them they propelled him forward; he went like a sleepwalker, his arms half out before him. From his desk by the door the attendant watched and smiled encouragingly.

In the hallway they found an unoccupied nook, bright with sunshine, and sat down. Mary Margaret clutched her pocketbook until her knuckles whitened and said, "Wilroy, I declare, he looks older."

"Now, I don't know," Wilroy said, gently. "He looks a little fatter."

"Pshaw!" Mary Margaret said. "It's in his eyes. That's where you can tell." Her voice broke.

"Now, I don't know," Wilroy said, but he did not look at Jake's face.

"Well, I know," Mary Margaret said. "And when your heart's broke, it don't ever heal. That hangdog look's not ever going to go away. Remember Mattie Perkins when her little girl got run over? She had the same look, and it never went away although she had four more kids afterward. Jake's look isn't ever going to go away either. You mark my words."

Wilroy stood up and said, "I tell you what. I'm going to go get us some ice-cream cones in that snack shop and bring 'em back here."

Ice cream. He had loved it so much and knew the word. Mary Margaret looked at him, but he showed no response. Her mouth tightened; her belief strengthened. Something that had been alive in Jake, that made him go, had gone out of him. She knew it. He seemed almost a stranger to her. It was as if he knew too much now, things he never was supposed to know. Strange places and strange ways. She looked out onto the patio at the strange world there of patients and attendants, and she felt herself a long way from home. At last she knew the answer to the question she and Wilroy had asked themselves over and over, and she moved her lips and said to herself without sound, He never should have been taken from home. She wondered what he was going to do when he went back. They were all going to have to make the best of things. When Wilroy returned she brightened and was gay and passed around the ice-cream cones and said they were having a party. But before the end of it, she knew even Wilroy saw the difference in Jake.

"Well, it's bus time," she said, eventually. "You better take him and wash him up. He's covered with ice cream."

Jake sensed they were leaving, and she saw his face change. When they got up, he did too. She held him to her a moment and said, "Oh, if only he could tell us. If only he could tell his Mary

Margaret. Mary Margaret loves you, honey. She's thinking of you and praying for you."

She released him and stepped back. She felt tears coming and knew this time she would not be able to check them. She hurried away and turned back once and cried out so terribly that several people passing in the hall turned and looked at her, "Oh, tell him! Tell him he's coming home, Wilroy!"

Wilroy gripped his arm, not knowing what to do. The attendant, who had been watching from behind the window, came out and said, "I'll take care of him if you want to go on."

Wilroy said, in a tentative way, "I was going to wash his hands." He nodded at them.

The attendant caught Jake's hands in his and said, "Did you have ice cream? Nice, huh?" He led him away. Jake looked over his shoulder, not understanding.

"You're coming home, boy!" Wilroy shouted.

He stood in the hall, embarrassed, because people came even out of doors to look at him. But more, he was frightened because he had failed. He wanted to run after Jake, grip him by the shoulders and tell him over and over and over again, if need be, that he was coming home. He had to understand. He, Wilroy, had to absolve himself, partly, of his share of the blame for what had happened to Jake. Surely he and Mary Margaret had not tried hard enough. Surely there was something they could have done.

He thought he would cry too. He turned away, himself feeling like the broken, almost old man that Jake had been as he was led away. It had been in his face, as Mary Margaret said, and in his walk and in the droop of his shoulders. He thought for a moment of the way Jake had been before: free, in his own way, proud. Wilroy's shoulders drooped even further, his walk was even more shuffling, and he went off down the hall looking for Mary Margaret.

I I

Jake's month was up early in November, and before sunup on a Sunday morning, Wilroy and Mary Margaret drove back to get him. They expected to return again just after dark. They chose Sunday because all their lives on Sunday nights town had been as deserted as some old Western ghost town. People only passed through on their way to evening service, wherever it was to be held. The two churches, Methodist and Baptist, alternated holding service on Sunday nights; not enough people attended to make it worth while heating two churches or having two sermons written. Then, when church was over about eight o'clock, they passed back through, leaving their dust to fall silently on the deserted road.

But the day played a trick on Wilroy and Mary Margaret. It was a cold, fine, brilliant day, and the sun seemed to have frozen in the sky. It remained a round, hard, blinding object just at eye level long past the time it should have sunk. Then it seemed only to diminish slowly until it was the size of a pin prick, and you could squint and your eye could contain the sun itself. When all its roundness was gone, and there was only a yellow mellowness in the sky where it had been, it sent back, as an afterthought, a sundown that was mauve and rose. Shading their eyes, people looked at it and speculated that tomorrow it was going to snow.

When Wilroy and Mary Margaret drove into town, with Jake in the back seat, the glow fell on them. Mary Margaret had lowered the sunshade as they drove into the sun. Now she lifted it, and a sound escaped her involuntarily.

"Wilroy, did they come just to stare?" she said. Way in the back of her mind an old fear stirred. She had always wanted to believe that most folks were good Christian people with all good intentions, and now here were the store porches as crowded as midweek to belie it.

"They ought to be horsewhipped," he said. Glancing about, he saw some of his own friends, and a part of him shut off from them, forever.

Mary Margaret was nervous and did not know whether to turn and look at Jake or not. When she did, he was only sitting straight, staring straight ahead as he had been doing the whole trip. But there was a glisten to his lips that would have been saliva if he had opened his mouth.

His hair had been freshly cut (there was some-

thing infinitely touching to Mary Margaret about
the closely clipped sides, so neat to his head, the
hairs closest to his cheeks stiff and short and
lighter, almost like new hair; like a child tidied
for his first appearance somewhere, school or Sunday school, he would not look the remainder of
the year as altogether presentable as he did now);
he was freshly shaved and bathed, and he wore
overalls so stiff in their brand-newness that the bib
stood away from his shirt as if it were stuffed with
something. She looked at his hands and thought
how wrong it was that they should be so pale; the
good color he kept all year had faded, and his
hands had the unfortunate appearance of having
accepted the last month's idleness. They lay
cupped, palms up, at the creases where his thighs
were attached to his body. His eyes met hers a
moment, and she would have sworn that he almost
smiled before he looked again at the road, his
eyes having taken in once, flickered and turned
away from, the people on the store porches. She
was positive that he knew where he was, just as
she had been positive from his behavior when they
first put him into the car that he knew where he
was going. She and Wilroy had wanted to rein-
troduce him to home quietly, without any kind of
fuss. They would stay with him the first night, and
Jurldeane would come every day for the first week.

No one had objected when they heard Jake was
coming home. Time had passed; they had gotten

everything off their chests once; everyone felt better: the underdog knew where he stood. They had been assured, through reports of medical reports, that Jake was not dangerous; he was not a criminal and not really insane, else they would have kept him at the state hospital, wouldn't they? Think of it more that he's sick and can't be cured. Oh, sick. Sick, they could grasp. They would probably keep a closer eye on the children than before. Perhaps they would feel in their hearts a little less kindly. But if the boy were only sick . . . Why, he was one of their own, after all! Come to think of it, Jake's people had been in these parts near 'bout as long as anybody's. Many people could remember his grandfather, and some his great-grandfather. Remember the old Darby place? It hadn't been quite so down-in-the-mouth as what they had come to. Too bad his daddy had died so early, too bad Jud had gone off like that. Now Jake, he never had gone to do any harm.

But they wanted to see him. And some, without knowing it, had arrived expecting to see more than they saw: Wilroy and Mary Margaret driving through town with Jake sitting upright in the back seat. They had come with the same feeling of expectancy with which they drove to Memphis twice a year, in May to the Cotton Carnival parade and again in December to the Christmas parade.

"Is that him!" a little girl cried, and it could have been Santa Claus in the final float of the latter parade, only her mother said, "Hush."

"Evenin'," several people said, with sheepish grins, when Wilroy drew alongside them to turn off the main road.

The car windows were closed, and Mary Margaret turned a deaf ear and kept her grim face straight ahead. She peeped sideways at Wilroy and saw his mouth corners turned down; his nose had the blanched, tweaked look it always had when he was angry.

Now the road plunged downward so steeply as to make Mary Margaret gasp; then they were out of sight of town, and only the dark tops of trees with a swath between told the townspeople where the car had gone.

They all turned and looked at one another after the car disappeared. Not knowing exactly what they had expected, they did not know whether they had seen it or not. They did not know whether they were disappointed or not.

"Well, what'd you think?"

"How'd you think he looked?"

They turned to one another, questioning. Some said they hadn't seen him well enough; others said he looked exactly the same, and those right next to them said, No, he looked different; he was older-looking, or something. Then there seemed no more to say, and they began to disperse. All they could have agreed on, if anyone had mentioned it, was the silence that had prevailed as he was driven through town. In it they had heard only the church bell, which had been tolling for some time in vain. Now, hearing it again, those who had parked their cars along the road to wait started up their motors and drove off to worship, quite late.

When Wilroy stopped the car before Jake's house, he and Mary Margaret did not have to tell him to get out. He was already trying the door handle when Mary Margaret turned and reached over the back seat and opened the door for him. She would have followed, but Wilroy put out a restraining hand. "Let him go by hisself," he said. She patted Wilroy's arm, thinking she should have thought of that.

He went at an unaccustomed fast pace and stopped only once to watch a blackbird fly overhead. *Caw caw* it cried while he watched, and he almost put out his hand, but then he did not. He hunched his shoulders and lowered them and went on. His house had never been locked; there was no key. Opening the door, he went inside and closed the door behind him. Mary Margaret and Wilroy sat on until full dark came and a candle was lit indoors. Then they went inside, too.

He was sitting at the table, the candle before him, eating. He was in the act of spreading butter on his bread; his mouth was full and chewing; it ceased, his hands, holding the knife and bread before him, stilled, and his eyes opened in total surprise.

Mary Margaret and Wilroy stood with their rolled-up nightclothes, their toothbrushes inside, feeling as foolish as if they had walked into any stranger's suppertime without knocking. At Mary Margaret's side her handbag hung heavy, full of little glass jars wrapped in tissue paper to protect them and also because they were irrevocably greasy. They contained her going-to-bed creams. Immediately she saw herself choosing them, wrapping them, drying her toothbrush, and she had to laugh, though she did not think the moment warranted it. Beside her she felt Wilroy let go like a punctured balloon, and he laughed too.

Jake, having begun to chew again, looked as if he knew that whatever the moment had been, it had passed. He grinned too, rocking back and forth in his chair in time to his chewing.

Wilroy drew his hand across his mouth and said, "Well, boy, it looks to me like you weren't expectin' no company tonight. What say, Miz Sheaffer?"

"Well, I reckon you're right," Mary Margaret said; but she felt sad, like a mother unneeded. She glanced around the room at what he had been doing while they were outside. Yesterday she had brought in food and cleaned and arranged the house, and knew everything's place. He had sat on every chair and on the bed; the imprint of his bottom was on the cushions and on the bedspread. He had looked into all the cabinets; the doors stood slightly open. He had gone to the back windows and looked out; she had left the shades half drawn, now they were all the way up. He had put away the few belongings he had; the box in which he had brought them home was empty on the floor beside him.

"Well, I reckon this boy's going to take care of hisself like he's always done," Wilroy said. He was restless and ready to go since they were not going to stay. His fingers drummed on the doorframe.

"All right," Mary Margaret said. "We're going." She crossed the room and put her hand on Jake's shoulder. "Good night, honey. Good night."

"You come uptown tomorrow, you hear?" Wilroy said. "Town!" His hand made a vague gesture; he could not think how to describe town with it, and Jake seemed not to understand as once he would have. His eyes remained on Wilroy, steady and expressionless. "Town!" Wilroy said. "Town!"

"Wilroy, hush," Mary Margaret said. "Maybe he's forgotten the word, but he won't forget to come. Bye-bye, now, honey, bye-bye." She almost bent and kissed the top of his head but did not. She crossed the room and she and Wilroy left, closing the door without looking back. They were glad not to be spending the night, though neither confessed it, even to the other.

"Well, what do you think?" Mary Margaret said

when the car was started and they were again on the road. Feeling quite tired, she leaned her head back.

"About what?" Wilroy said.

"Why, about Jake. I mean, do you think he's going to be lonely?"

"Lonely? He'll be uptown tomorrow. I've never known uptown to be lonely, except on Sundays, and I'm not sure about that any more. He spends the better part of his time up there. He'll be all right."

"Well, he's used to having folks around him all the time now, and there's nobody here to look in on him but us and Loma and Jurldeane, and Lord knows, we all got other things to do too, especially with Christmastime coming. I declare to my soul, it's a shame about Ruth Edna. She'd be the one to spend the time with him."

Ever since the night Jake ran amuck, the mention of his name or of anything that had happened to him that night threw Ruth Edna off. She would cry and sigh and gulp and tremble. Though, Cotter said, she was nervous as a witch all the time and cried if you asked her what time it was. Did anybody realize what he was having to put up with? People certainly realized it was hard trying to carry on a conversation with her. She never finished one sentence before she started another, so that you could never be sure you were exactly sure you knew what she was talking about. All she could offer as excuse was that she was "blue," just "blue all the time."

Do you think it's *possible*, some of the women queried each other, that Ruth Edna's just *now* having the change?

And poor Hattie—with the loss of Ruth Edna's wits she was even more lonely. She had given up completely the idea of marrying Cotter, and that same fateful night when so much else had happened the rooster had died. In the time since, Hattie had worked it around in her mind to being the town's fault. If everyone else had not run that night to see Jake, she would not have; thus, at the crucial moment, she would have been there with a drop of whisky or to reapply his mustard plaster. She had turned to the Bible for succor and prayed alone nightly before the little fire it had taken all her strength to build. Forgive 'em, for they didn't know what they was doing. They had killed him, her only companion.

She had tried to explain it once to Mary Margaret, who had said, "Why, Hattie, I declare. It was a rooster. Only a bantam rooster."

Passing Hattie's now, seeing her little light far back off the road, Mary Margaret thought of that time and wondered what was the matter with everybody; was everybody losing their faculties?

Why, she had almost run over that bird in the road once, a long time ago. She wondered what in the world Hattie would have thought of her then.

She had looked aghast enough just because Mary Margaret said, "After all, it's not like it was a *child.*"

It seemed everybody was acting strange lately. She said as much to Wilroy, but she might as well have been talking to herself. Wilroy was hungry and he was tired of driving; he was not looking for any conversation.

Sighing, Mary Margaret thought she had even felt a lot different herself this past month. She was often depressed too, and she went around with a great feeling of disappointment. She had not been quite sure what the disappointment was about. But now, sighing even more heavily, she admitted that it was just about people, people in general.

12

It did not snow the following day, and Jake did not come to town. He did not come that whole first week while Jurldeane was there, though she tried to persuade him. He stayed in the house mostly, finally ventured to the porch and then went to the yard and began to feed the chickens, which Wilroy had kept while he was gone and now returned. People said they bet he would come once he was by himself again, but when he had not appeared by Wednesday of the following week, they began going to see him. They took jars full of homemade chicken-and-rice soup and coconut cake, as if they expected to find him in bed, sick. But there he was, up and around, the same as always, except he seemed withdrawn and older and paler. But he'd put a little meat on his bones, hadn't he? they consoled themselves.

Gradually they stopped going, thinking still that he would come to town. But when he did not, they said it was probably just as well. They would have forgotten him really, except that Wilroy and Mary Margaret and Miss Loma did not let them. One of the two women was always approaching another woman to say, Why don't you fix up a little cake or a pot of stew for me to take to Jake? Or Wilroy would point out to a man that something or other he had on was looking a little worn; why didn't he give it to Jake?

With these constant reminders, they would have to remember and would have to ask themselves again, Did we do right? Then, for fear that they had not, they would give Wilroy the shirt off their back, or go home and put the stew meat on to simmer.

Of all the people around, Little T. was probably the only one unaware of Jake's return. He never went to town on Sunday and when cold weather came on seldom left the bottomland at all. He knew what happened to Jake the night after he saw him in the road, and surely as a trap springing, his mind closed over the fact that Ruth Edna had something to do with it. When he returned the following Thursday with the medicine, he had been more sure of it than ever. The woman who came to the screen and took the medicine was not the woman who had given him the money the week before. He would have sworn on his momma's and daddy's graves, both, that her hair had turned white in a week. Before, it had been a gray-and-brown mixture, but that night it stood up around her face wild-looking and white. Perhaps it was a reflection of her face, for that was as white as if she had painted it to be a clown. Her lips were a dark, cold purple, as if stained with Grape-ade, and were narrower and thinner-looking. He handed her the paper sack wordlessly, stepped back and would have made tracks for home, but she said, "Little T., come back soon as you can."

"Yes 'um," he said. "Yes 'um." And he knew if he had met a ghost in the graveyard he would not have been any more miserable than he was confronting Miss Ruth Edna that night.

He had been holed up in the bottomland since then, happy to be alone, happy not to have to tramp to town in the cold and happy not to have had any truck with Miss Ruth Edna since then. But how was he going to get the lure? He was sitting on his porch this early December day, huddled into his old Army jacket, trying to think of a better, also quicker, way. He felt sorry for himself. Didn't a man deserve a little seventy-five-cents' worth of something at Christmastime? There was nobody who was going to give it to him, no Santa Claus in his life. The only person who was going to look after Little T. was Little T.

He was surprised himself at the way his thoughts had persisted all these months, until it seemed now he had to have the lure, no matter what. Even, he had decided, if he had to take the money off somebody. Shoot, to some folks seventy-five cents was nothing. Yet you could not go up and ask them for the money. That was the system, screwy as it was. Life. Phew.

He had been thinking of people he could take the money from, who wouldn't miss it: Miss Loma, Mister Wilroy, anybody who owned a store, and preachers. He believed firmly that all preachers kept their hand in the till. But there was a very good reason he could not rob any of these people: he was scared to.

He had a piece of kindling wood in his hand and he began to whittle. He whittled all morning, and it was long about noon he realized that what he had been whittling was a small gun. He looked at it lying in the flat of his hand. Then he thrust it into his coat pocket and went inside. Standing before the broken piece of glass over his washstand, he said, "Put 'em up. Hand over seventy-five cents."

He said it over and over in various imitative ways, using voices he had heard on the radio and in the movies. He was firm in his decision not to steal more than he needed for the lure. It made him feel not so guilty. He said it so many times that finally he could hear himself off from himself and he told himself the truth. The whole thing was too silly to think about. Nobody was going to hold up somebody for that little. But just suppose he did. Then, the next thing, he walks into Miss Loma's and plops down that amount for the lure. Every-one would know it was him had done it.

He thought of robbing a house off somewhere. In summer he could do it. But in winter people stayed home, kept their windows closed tight and were liable to lock their doors when they left. Still, that seemed the only possibility, a house off by itself somewhere. He thought of robbing Miss Loma's store, right there on the main road of town, and he thought he'd cream his pants standing in his own house, it made him so afraid. He could not do it. Who lived off? He thought of Mister Metcalf, and he thought of his collection of rifles that was famous the whole county and more, and he gave up that idea. If only he could find out somebody who was going up to Memphis for a day's Christ-mas shopping, he would have it made. For once, it was convenient to be colored; he would wear dark clothes and no one would see him even if the moon came full.

He would not carry the gun; it was too risky. If he got caught later, and it was known he had car-ried a gun, no one would want to believe it had been a toy. They would want to make it out as bad as they could. He was not in any particular favor in town right now anyway. For the heck of it only, he had not long ago referred to a white man, in public, by his first name. A white man, overhear-ing, had said, "Boy, I believe you mean Mister Bill, don't you?"

"Yes, suh, I believe I do," he had said, without malice.

Later on Bald Dave had said, "You got rocks in your head? You want to get us all in Dutch?" And in her store one day, Miss Loma said casually, with a hint of warning, "Little T., you need a job to keep your mind occupied."

He had not observed any particular unfriendliness in town, only a certain air of watchfulness. He knew what people said was, "If ever there is any trouble here, Little T.'ll be one of the ones that starts it."

Today, after his noon dinner, he started off to town to get some coffee, a supply he had forgotten to lay by. When he had not gone far, he heard behind him the crackling of dry winter branches on the ground and, turning, saw Stump, his friend who had had three fingers shot off in a dynamite accident, coming along with a gun and a brace of quail over his shoulder.

"Wait on me," Stump called.

When he came up, Little T. said, "Boy, what you doing sneaking around?"

"Sneaking?" Stump said. "I was just walking like I walk. What's the matter with you? You jumped like you been shot when you heard me."

"Just got something on my mind," Little T. said. He looked at the birds. "Where you been? I ain't heard no shooting this morning."

"I been way on through the bottom and clear to

the other side," Stump said. "Some good shooting." They came out of the bottom and reached the road, and indicating his old truck pulled to one side, Stump said, "Hop in. I'll give you a ride."

"Much obliged," Little T. said. He pulled himself up to the running board and got in. The truck was a Model A, with seating benches built opposite each other in its open bed. Everyone called it The Whoopee. The floorboard on Little T.'s side was missing. He had to balance one foot the best he could; the other he put out on the running board. He braced himself in the truck by holding on to the windshield frame. He looked down at the road speeding by where his feet should have been, and when gravel flew up, he threw it back again. Cold rushed around his head and stung his eyes, blistered his ears. Conversation was impossible until they stopped in front of Miss Loma's. Then, feeling his fingers frozen into their bent position around the windshield frame, Little T. said, "Cold."

"Good bird weather," Stump said.

Little T. got down and said again, "Much obliged."

"Come see us," Stump said, and drove off. He looked for a moment into the rear-view mirror and waved, and Little T. waved back.

Miss Loma was nowhere to be seen; her daughter was tending store. When Little T. entered, she was talking to another woman, and it was as if he had not come in at all. She kept right on talking, though

224

the other woman had completed her purchases. She was holding a large grocery bag and looked as if she had been trying for some time to edge her way out of the store. Frances, having just learned she and Billy were to have another baby, was bitter. "I'm telling you thirty-one years old's too old to have another baby."

"Oh, go on, Frances," the other woman said. "You got years to have two or three more kids."

"That's what you think," Frances said, slowly, as if she would kill her with words, thrown like knives, if she could.

Little T. had stood in the background, waiting, patient, his eyes averted; now he glanced up in surprise, her voice was so harsh, so full of a hateful sound. She caught him looking and said, "You want something, boy?"

"Yes, ma'm, pound o'percolatin'."

"Credit, I guess," she said. She moved along behind the counter and took down the coffee.

"Yes, 'um."

She did not look at him but wrote his name in a book, and he took the can from the counter. Meanwhile the other woman had edged her way all the way to the door, and now she said, "Well, you just got to make the best of it, Frances. It'll be over before you know it."

"Oh yes, just six years after it's finally born and it'll be off to school. I can hardly wait."

"Well, I got to run along," the other woman said

hurriedly, opening the door. Before closing it she looked around and said, "Still seems funny in here without Jake sitting by the stove."

"Lonesome in here," Frances said. The mention of Jake's name made her start, as if the life in her had already quickened.

"You reckon he'll come back to town in the spring?" the woman said.

"I don't know," Frances said. She did not want to talk about Jake and showed it; it made her feel the same as the morning sickness she had had earlier.

"Bye-bye," the woman said.

"Come back to see us," Frances said. The woman closed the door, and Frances looked at Little T. and said, "You want something else?"

"No'm, I was just looking at that lure," he said. He indicated his coffee and said, "I thank you." He went to the door and opened it. "Miss Loma sick?"

"Got a cold," Frances said. She had gone back along the counter to her chair near the cash register. She sat down and picked up her knitting.

"Oh," Little T. said. He started to close the door.

"Come back to see us," Frances said, automatically.

"I thank you," Little T. said. He closed the door.

The loony man. Why hadn't he thought of him? Little T. stood on the store porch breathing in the crisp, cold day. Even that white man would have at least seventy-five cents to his name laying around. They'd dragged him off so quick, his house was liable to be just as he'd left it. It would be easy to rob. And he was away. Man, that man was gone and had been for a month or more. Nobody watched his house. There it was, just sitting out there by itself, a house to rob if ever there was a house. Cold went right through Little T. as if he had on no clothes at all. But he thought he could do it. There seemed so little risk. He began to plan.

At eight o'clock he came again out of the bottom, braced with coffee, wide awake, trembling. A car went by just as he reached the road and he fell to the bank and hugged it far beyond a reasonable length of time, until he was thoroughly chilled and knew that tomorrow he would have a sore throat; he could already feel the first faint scratchy tickle way down; he swallowed two or three times.

He thought he could still hear music from the car's radio floating across the countryside, but the car had been gone too long. It was fear, only fear that he heard, louder than the music ever had been. Cautiously he went up the bank and peeped over into the road, and from the treetops on the other side the moon peeped back. Go home, it said. It was white and full: too full. He could see everything as clearly as if it were dawn. The road ahead, the gravel, the little cabins of cedarwood were white as chalk. Washing machines on their porches were great white hulks. He left the main gravel road, crossed a moon-washed field and entered a soft dust road, the dust shooting ahead of him in soft white puffs, that would take him a back way. He saw families inside their cabins, and it gave him a great sickening feeling that he was so alone here in this white and silent world, even in the real world. He had never realized before how alone he was. Who had chosen his lonely way? Not him; he would not have chosen it for anything in the world.

He came to a pond and skirted it and could see his figure, elongated and wavery, as he did so. He heard frogs croaking deep in their bellies. Too bad he didn't have a shotgun. *Blam*. There was nothing he liked better than frog legs so fresh they were still hopping in the skillet. Why had he never thought of hunting frogs here before? Perhaps it was premonition that told him he never would now, that he would never see this pond again.

His feet echoed hollowly against the cold wood of the man's front porch. The unlocked door creaked open on cold hinges. He entered and saw a kerosene lamp burning so low it was no more than a waver. It was sitting on a rickety table. Beside it was a white plate, an unfinished meal on it. The man sat in a chair beside the table and looked at it. Why, Little T. wondered, hadn't anybody told him the man was home again? It seemed everybody in the world had ganged up to play one giant mean trick on him, and his feelings were hurt; he wanted to cry.

The man turned and looked at him and something crossed his face. Perhaps it was surprise; it was not fear, and Little T. was sorry that it was not. For his own fear was in the room, as large, as ominous as the world. He hardly knew what to do with it. He took a step forward, and he took two steps back. He felt that whatever had guided him wrongly along life was going to guide him now. If it took him to the door, he would open it and leave. Otherwise, he would stay. Now he was rooted to the spot.

Around the flickering wick the room was a cavern of darkness. The room beyond was also a great dark cave, with a tiny candle burning in a saucer on a bureau. Suddenly Little T. was walking toward it. He brushed right by the man, doing so. The man did not even turn. He merely continued to look at what was before him: the table, the lamp, the unfinished food on the white plate. It was as if he knew full well now that whatever was his was not.

Little T. began to search the bureau drawers, but he could see nothing. When he picked up the saucer, tallow dripped onto his hand and burned it; it was a nuisance to hold the saucer while he searched. He looked around the room and found a kerosene lamp without a shade sitting in a corner of the room. It was full of coal oil, and he set it on top of the bureau and lighted it from the candle. He searched again and found nothing. All of the drawers stuck, and he had to slam them to shut them again. Two of them were empty. One contained old clothes that seemed to have belonged to a woman. One held candle ends and rubber bands and all sorts of odds and ends. He was just going through the bottom drawer—there were some boxes in it and he was opening those—when he heard someone behind him. He whirled around, overwhelmed by fear, even when he saw it was only Jake. The man was older than he, but much taller; perhaps he was powerful; Little T. didn't know. At the moment of his turning, he kicked the drawer to. The lamp slid backward and off the bureau and down the wall, spilling kerosene and igniting it. The wallpaper had long been browned and stained and torn, but once the pattern had been clusters of pink roses and trailing ivy. It was dusty and ignited quickly. Dust was everywhere, catching fire. Fire ran helter-skelter, igniting curtains, a bedspread, a rag rug—the entire room. In a few moments, they could barely breathe. Tears burst from Little T.'s eyes: tears from the fire, but tears of rage and sorrow. He opened his mouth to yell at Jake and found he could not talk. Fumes from the fire rushed down his gullet. Smoke choked him. He was finally able to cry, "Git out. *Git!*"

But Jake would not move. Little T. beat on him with his fists, never thinking of leaving him. Jake only stared, and Little T. was so close he could see the flames reflected, leaping, in his eyes. He gasped again, begging, "Git!"

Jake turned and started for the door. Little T. watched him slowly sink down, feather-light, and stretch out full-length, overcome. There was something of disbelief, still, on his face.

Little T. started forward and found himself on fire. He cried out horribly, terribly, and fell on the floor and rolled, beating upon himself until his hands were torture. The flames went out but the pain, he knew, was more than he could bear. He made his way to Jake and caught his suspenders between his teeth. He put one scorched arm across his back and fitted a hand beneath his armpit; his other hand he fitted beneath Jake's nearer armpit. Somehow, on one hip, drawing his legs up into a position of cramp, then straightening them, he dragged them both out of the room, into the next, where the air was better, and so on out the front door. Once they were on the porch, with super-human effort he gave Jake a shove that sent him rolling off the porch. He fell the short distance to the ground, rolled a little, and was clear of the fire—at least, Little T. thought, and prayed that he was not already dead.

He sent himself the same way and rolled a short distance away from Jake. Then he lost consciousness. When he opened his eyes again, he first saw the great fire. He knew he was dead and in Hell. "Man, I'm humble," he whispered.

Then he turned his head and saw the moon,

peaceful and calm, smiling down at him. He had to go home. That was all he knew, that he had to go home.

He knew that he had been hot, very hot. But now he felt frozen. Far away, there was a dull ache to his body. He stood up and walked a few yards in complete possession of himself, then he collapsed and knew he was hurt and sick and could not walk again as he had just done. But he had to go home.

He heard in the distance a bell ringing. He dragged himself in a fashion like a snake across the cold ground. He heard screams and a great many voices in the distance. He had to go home.

"I got to go home," he said, in almost a cry.

He dragged himself across a field prickly with dry grass. Sometimes he was in pain; sometimes he was not. Sometimes he felt as if layers of his skin were coming off. He went down a soft dust road and oh, it was soft and cool; he thanked God for it. He dragged himself in all positions on his knees, on his sides, on his elbows and using the backs of his wrists as hands. Always going home.

He saw cabins, most of them darkened now. He saw white appliances on their front porches. Then he knew the pierce of gravel and could stand it only because he knew it meant he was almost home. Then he was rolling down his own bank. He was in the bottomland. He could die safe, in his own place, with some dignity, not like he would have died if they had caught him. He had killed a man, was what he had done. Bless Jesus, his momma and daddy never had lived to know.

He knew he was dying. I suffered to come unto Thee, he whispered. Lemme walk on God's highway, please, suh.

He crawled along wondering if he had done all this for seventy-five cents. He thought of how he had left this peaceful place only a few hours ago, never dreaming of the misery this night would turn into.

He had thought he would go into his cabin to die. But instead he pulled himself up against his tree near the creek—he could hear its peaceful night sound; he could see his cabin faintly in the moonlight. He leaned against the tree and looked about.

His end had come. He huddled to the tree, overwhelmed by darkness. He tried to think of one last word, but he no longer had anything to say to this world. He thought of what he wanted to tell his daddy. "You had a fish on your line that last day when I pulled it in!"

It would tickle the old man to pieces.

13

Nothing surprised Jake any more. He had been taken away and returned; the taking away had changed him. He had left home; it would never be the same again.

His life had been so full for a while that he could not think. But now that he was away from the other place, he could remember it. He remembered faces, voices, names. And he remembered his bed, for all he had come to want to do was lie on it. Then only, when sleep came, or night, could he find the silence that was him. Then he would remember home and know that was where he belonged.

Now he was home, and it was not the same.

In the other place he had missed his road and his trees and his house, the coo of the pigeons nesting in the eaves. But now that he had come back to them they did not seem the same.

In the other place he had remembered town, and it was a mixture of memories, but the most vivid was as the place where he had had to run and run and run, though gradually the reason for it had faded and was no longer clear. It was the same as when he had had to clap his hands over his ears and run breathlessly from the little boys shouting after him, beating horribly with rocks on tin pails. He knew the safe place was away from them. Sometimes now his loneliness tugged him toward town, but a stronger instinct kept him away.

He saw the stranger in his doorway without surprise. Only the fire surprised him. He had not known there could be a fire of such size. He tried to confine it to the fireplace, but it would not stay. It continued to leap around the room, touching the chairs, the bed, the walls, the floor, until finally he realized that it could touch him.

Then he turned and walked away. He could not breathe. He walked away lightly, into darkness.

14

Miss Alma, waking in the night thirsty, saw the fire. She ran straight into the road and began tolling the bell. Homer Brown, the closest, waked at the first *clunk*, before she even got it going good. Looking out, he called, "Alma, go get your wrapper and shoes. You'll freeze."

By then someone else arrived and took over the tolling. And soon the rope was given to children; grownups were needed for the bucket brigade. Long after everything that could be done for the fire had been done, and the tragedy discovered, the bell was still ringing.

Red Anderson, grimy and tired from digging a trench around the fire, leaned on his shovel and called, "For the Lord's sake, somebody go get them kids off that rope."

Frances Morgan said she would and went off in the middle of her mother's telling her it was too long a climb back. But because of her condition she had lifted no buckets and done no other work and was not worn out like everyone else, except those who had been too old to do anything; and they were also too old to go back.

Because of the great distance to town all the able women had had to join this bucket brigade and, in some cases, had had to double up in order to hand on the full buckets. The fire had been at its height when discovered, and it was hopeless to save anything, and everyone soon knew it. All they wanted then was to keep it from spreading. Men, bent double, swatted at its edges with feed sacks, and others, with Red directing them, dug the trench around it, their faces as red as the fire, their eyes almost blinded.

Going back, Frances followed the remnants of the brigade. Homer had given the word to stop. "All right, all right, we've done all we can do." And the order had been passed along back to town, to the pump, where the teenage boys were taking turns. Freddie Moore had been pumping when word came, and he let go with a suddenness and sank onto his haunches with a stomach-ache. All along the way people had dropped where they stood, in attitudes of exhaustion, and except for that might have been picnicking on the grass if it were summertime.

And they were quiet; they only sat and watched the men beating and digging. Their buckets were where they had set them down, some of them full, some of them empty; and some of them remained there a very long time, forgotten. When the owners eventually went back, of course, the water in them was skimmed with ice.

Frances made her way without speaking, and no one spoke to her. After the hubbub when the fire was newly discovered, the silence now seemed even more overwhelming. The fire was under control, and when Frances looked back, she saw that the men beating and digging were not doing it frantically as before, but slowly and methodically, and tiredly, too. Going in a circle around the fire, they seemed to be performing some old Indian ritual, and their figures, dark as silhouettes, made grotesque, dancelike movements.

Turning, she saw Kate French, newly relieved of child, resting, her bucket beside her, and she thought, It's too soon for her to have been doing that.

Kate, catching her eye, motioned, and Frances went to her and bent over in the dark, and they whispered as if someone were still dying. "Is he dead, for sure?" Kate said.

Frances bit her lip and nodded. Tears sprang simultaneously to both their eyes. "Pitiful," Kate said.

When Frances went on, she wondered why Kate had risked overstraining herself. Not long ago she had been the one dead set, more than anyone else, that Jake must be sent away. Those who had fought the fire had not known for some time that Jake was dead; and there had been plenty of people just to keep the fire from spreading. It was for Jake that Kate had worked and not from a sense of guilt either. There was a finality to her pronouncement: "Pitiful." That was all the thinking about it she and most of the townspeople would ever do. Frances knew that for sure. That was just the way folks were, take 'em or leave 'em. If she had not felt so uncertain of her own character, she would certainly want to leave them alone. But with all her own deeper suffering over Jake, had she helped him any?

When she reached the bell shed, several little girls stood in a corner howling; they had not had a turn. All the little boys, swinging and yelling like Tarzan, possessed the rope at once. Rescuing it, Frances gave each little girl a turn, then sent everybody where he was expected: home or to the fire.

Homer, Buck French and several other men passed her now, loaded down with dark-looking bundles; they were blankets and blanket rolls, and she thought she saw the glinting aluminum legs of a folding cot. Two or three men would have to spend the night near the fire; the other blankets were for Jake to be carried away in.

Her mother had found him shortly after everyone had begun to fight the fire. When Frances arrived, her mother was cradling his head in her lap. She had looked up, her face full of tears, and said, "Look. He appears to be smiling."

"Oh, blessed," little Miss Hattie had said, huddling near Miss Loma and also crying.

And Frances remembered now that Miss Ruth Edna had been there, too. In body, she thought; no telling where her mind is. I guess she's lucky. She doesn't have sense enough left to have to think about her guilt, like Frank and me.

In the midst of the night's work, she had caught Frank's eyes on her. By then everyone knew of Jake's death, and looking at her, Frank's eyes had held a startled, turned-inward look; probably like the one in her own, she had thought, and her bitterness toward him had lessened a little.

Returning to the fire, she saw two figures struggling back up the hill, the bulky bundle of blanket between them swinging slightly. On the farthest reaches of the fire, people talked in whispers about where they were going. Some said to the church; others said to Brother Patrick's back room.

Billy was slumped on the ground exhausted, and she sat next to him, unnecessarily close, held his arm and whispered, "If it's a boy, let's name him after Jake."

He turned and looked at her. His face was streaked with dirt and in the fire's shadows appeared deeply lined and old. Ashes, settling on his hair, had turned it white. Startled, Frances felt her own youth.

"You don't want to do that," he said, his voice dry and wise. "You're upset and emotional."

240

She said, after a moment, "I guess you're right." She knew all people would remember was that she had named her child after an idiot.

His hand closed over hers and held it hard for what seemed like the first time. Her mother came by, deeply tired, Miss Hattie trailing behind. Despite her grief, Miss Loma's face brightened knowingly when she saw Frances and Billy together. She put her hand lightly on Frances' head in passing, not wanting to talk, saying all that was necessary.

"I'll tend store tomorrow, Mama," Frances called, her voice like a thin tinkle in the great dark starry night.

"We'll see," Miss Loma said. She stopped and turned around. "You need your rest too."

Frances was looking at the sky when her mother spoke, and she smiled as if someone were looking back at her. She thought of something she had learned long ago when a visiting Sunday-school superintendent had questioned her about the day's lesson, a lesson she had not prepared. "What is God, Frances?" he had said, while the teachers and children listened. She had been wearing long white wool socks, and as she broke into perspiration, her legs began to itch violently. Then suddenly, like a miracle, the page over which she had only run her eye appeared before her. Clear as day, the question and answer stood out. "God is love," she had said.

Billy said, "You'll get cold sitting here." They stood up.

Miss Loma said, "Hattie, where's Ruth Edna?"

Miss Hattie said, "Cotter's got her."

Frances saw them trudging up through the dark together, Mr. May leading Miss Ruth Edna by the hand.

"I declare, I'll tell you one thing," Miss Loma said. "That man's taken hold. Two-three months ago, I thought he wasn't long for this world. Now he's like a well man."

"Well, you know what they say," Miss Hattie said. "Folks do what they have to."

They were walking back through the dark now too, Frances and Billy after the two women. They came to the bottom of the hill and began to climb.

Miss Loma said, "If we don't make it, you-all give us a push from the rear."

Miss Hattie scurried forward and said in quick whispers, "Loma, Loma, hush."

"Oh now, Hattie," Miss Loma said. "Billy don't think nothing about us old women."

They all laughed but Hattie, then were abruptly silent, feeling the laughter unseemly when they thought of the night's events.

They reached the main road just as Wilroy and Mary Margaret came up by another path, struggling under a load of extra blankets. Billy hurried to help them. He took those Mary Margaret was carrying, and she said, "Billy, I don't know who all those belong to. I reckon we'll just take them home, and folks can come claim 'em tomorrow. Or they can go squat."

"Why Ma' Margaret," Miss Hattie said, having never heard Mary Margaret speak in anger before.

"Oh, don't Mary Margaret me. Don't Mary Margaret me. Anybody in this town, ever again. Except you, Loma," she called over her shoulder. She went off down the road crying audibly.

Wilroy looked at them. "Maybe I ought to apologize for her, but I guess I'm not."

"Oh, nobody has to be apologized to," Miss Loma said. "Everybody's upset tonight."

"It's not just tonight. She said 'ever again.' She meant it. We'd already talked about it. We just don't feel the same about this town any more."

"Oh, Wilroy. Are you going to move away?" Miss Hattie said.

"No ma'm. That's the dickens. We can't pick up from where we've lived all our lives now. But the way Miss Mary Margaret and me figure, there's two factions in this town from now on. There's us, and there's the majority of the other folks."

No one said anything. He said, "Well, Loma, we better get some sleep. All the arranging will be up to us tomorrow."

She sighed. "I'm sure of that."

"I got to go. Good night all," Miss Hattie said. Everyone said good night. "You want Billy to walk you home, Miss Hattie?" Frances said.

"Lord, no. I been walking home by myself over thirty years, and nothing's gotten me yet. Sometimes I wish something would." The little figure disappeared into the dark.

One by one lights had gone off in all the houses; the road was clear of people.

"Here. This boy and I better get on so he can get back and get some sleep," Wilroy said.

"Go on to bed, hon," Billy said. "I'll be right back." He leaned over the blankets in his arms and kissed Frances lightly on the forehead.

"Loma, you come on. We'll drop you off," Wilroy said.

Miss Loma kissed Frances and went off with the two men. "Oh yes," she said. "On top of everything else, the town'll be running over with folks tomorrow. I'll *have* to open the store."

But it was noon before town was crowded. It took that long for people to hear about the fire. The women who had been there got their children off to school in the morning and went back to sleep. Only the men who absolutely had to went to work, and for the first time since it had been her job, Miss Alma opened the post office late.

Hoyt Springfield was credited with spreading the word. He had a morning appointment in Coldwater and on the way there stopped and told some people picking cotton. Since it was their own field, they left it. They told their neighbors and anyone else they saw on their way to town. And by noon people had come from all over. They went in droves to the site. It had been so many years since there had been a big fire anywhere around that it was outside the experience of almost everyone. And they wanted the children to see.

"You see there, you. I been tellin' you what you were going to end up doing, playing with matches!"

"Are you going to leave that there coal oil lamp alone *now!*"

And having agreed and been released, all the children ran then to kick up as much dust as they could around the edges of the fire. It was too hot to get any closer. The center was still smoldering, one enormous pile of ashes. And everyone talked about the fire and its start and the death it had caused. No one could remember knowing anyone before who had burned to death, though they all had heard of someone or knew someone who knew someone —and they all had stories to tell. Finally they moved on back to town and then, standing around, indoors or out, they told the stories again. . . .

That day anybody at all who had any ideas about where Jud might be sent out inquiries or told Wilroy, and he did. They waited two days to no avail. Then on the fourth day after the fire, they held the funeral.

The ladies went into their yards and did their best, but all they could come up with was fewer than a dozen late-blooming roses. Then the men went deep into the country around and cut greenery, just as in a few weeks they would return to cut greenery for Christmas. And once the church was decorated with the cool dark-gleaming pine, and the strong dark sweet-smelling cedar, it made the roses pale by comparison, and at the last moment Miss Loma removed the vase. Later she put the roses on the grave and, of course, they died quickly. All the ladies stood at the back of the church, examining their handiwork, and said, "It *is* lovely!"

In the two days that Jud was being looked for, a few people had continued to go to the fire. They were not looking for anything. It was obvious there was nothing to find. They simply went and walked around it, and some even walked into it, and they poked. They had sticks or pieces of things from the fire, and they looked into the ashes and settled and unsettled them, poking until whatever it is that makes people poke at fires was answered, and then they would have quit, except that Stump, hunting in the bottomland, found Little T.

Of course, being burned, he was linked to the fire, and it gave them a mystery. People speculated about every conceivable thing, but no one could give much credence to the possibility that he had expected to *steal* anything from Jake. What would he steal?

On the seventh day after the fire, Little T. was buried. It was decided not to open the casket, which was a good thing since everyone was stuffed inside the church with the windows sealed shut against the cold weather and the stove going full blast.

Then people began going back to the fire site, and some even went to Little T.'s. At both places they just stood around and talked. The marshal and his deputies tried to find a trail Little T. might have taken between the two places, but they found nothing.

Christmas came and, busy with that, people began to forget.

In January they had the first heavy snow they had had in ten years. The ground was covered for three days, and in some shady places there were traces of snow even after two weeks. People went nowhere they did not have to.

By March, when they were sticking their noses outdoors and beginning to talk about robins, and from then on, the fire was a topic of conversation only when visitors came to town or people who had been away a long time returned and asked about it. Then they relished telling it, and they told it step by step until they reached the discovery of the dead Negro in the bottomland; then they threw up their hands and said, "Now what can you make of that?"

Where the fire had been, the ashes eventually blew away, and weeds grew up around the edges. It was a wide burned-out blackened place in the ground, too inconveniently located for anyone else ever to build there.

All that had remained of the original house the morning after the fire was the blackened bedsprings and the chimney. The bedsprings stayed until they were rusty, and at last children, having gotten up their nerve, came and carted them away.

Then only the chimney remained. It had been made by hand and was well built of good solid stone. It stood on for a great many years to come, alone against the sky, like a monument to something.

Joan Williams

was born in Memphis, Tennessee, in 1928.
After graduating from Bard College, An-
nandale-on-Hudson, New York, she lived
briefly in New Orleans and New York City.
She now lives with her husband and two
sons in Stamford, Connecticut. Miss Williams' short story, "Rain Later," was
awarded first prize in *Mademoiselle's* College Fiction Contest and was given honor-
able mention in *Best Short Stories, 1949*,
edited by Martha Foley and David Burnett.
A short story, also titled "The Morning and
the Evening," was published in *The Atlantic Monthly* as an *Atlantic* "First" in 1953.